THE GREAT GANGSTER

To Jacqueline,
Happy Birthday!!
Enjoy the book.

Peter Howe

A Novella By Peter Howe

THE GREAT GANGSTER

COPYRIGHT © 2019 BY PETER HOWE

ALL RIGHTS RESERVED.

THIS BOOK OR ANY PORTION THEREOF MAY NOT BE REPRODUCED OR USED IN ANY MANNER WHATSOEVER WITHOUT THE EXPRESS WRITTEN PERMISSION OF THE OWNER, EXCEPT FOR THE USE OF BRIEF QUOTATIONS IN A BOOK REVIEW.

COVER ILLUSTRATIONS AND BOOK DESIGN BY HEARTISAN CREATIONS.

FIRST PRINTING, 2019

ISBN-13: 9781794668881

Dedications

I would like to dedicate this book to my mother and sister, whose support is remarkable and unwavering. My best friend Stephen, who is more than a friend he may as well be family. My cousin Steven Reid, someone who may as well be an older brother. Rob, Steve, and Chris who are always great and I know always have my back. Also, I would like to dedicate this to my friend Ben who helped me through the last few years, whether it be reviewing manuscripts or helping me sell the books I have. I would also like to dedicate this book to everyone else who has supported my past work and who has helped me reach this point in my dream of being an author, where I have written and self-published four books with hopefully more coming in the future.

I would also like to thank Jennifer from Heartisan Creations for her hard work and innovation in assisting me with the interior and exterior cover designs of my first novella.

THE GREAT GANGSTER

A Novella By Peter Howe

History

One day a few months ago Harry Goodrich was in his office typing up a modification to next summer's business plan. Suddenly he received a phone call, it was from a voice he knew as 'Jay.' The voice said, "They're coming, the warrant is being printed now!"

Harry asked, "Really? What are they charging me with?"

Jay responded, "I don't know, they're being really hush-hush about the whole thing."

Harry said, "Thank you, I'll make sure I am here when they arrive, I wouldn't want them to think I was hiding."

As soon as the phone hung up Harry thought to himself, "I have a lot of work to do before they arrive."

Which they did less than two hours later, with multiple police cars, a SWAT van waiting down the street and several cameras from the news media. Harry gave up willingly, rolling his eyes at how overblown this production was. He had long feared this was coming but thought he had been too careful. He wondered what this would mean not only for him but for everyone.

The Saturday before the trial Harry had a meeting with his closest confidants, Brian his driver, Alicia his assistant, Kevin co-manager of his operations and Sophia the other co-manager of his operations.

Harry began, "As all of you know, Levine is coming down hard. We were lucky that he didn't get any hard data when he came to my office because it was in transit from one of several undisclosed locations when they struck. Things are going to get rough, our primary goal is to beat all these charges, but make no mistake, even if we beat them all, he will try again and we will have to be one step ahead of him."

Sophia looked at Alicia, who seemed slightly confused, before asking, "So where are the files now?"

Everyone looked at her, as Harry responded, "I moved them to another undisclosed location. The fact that he got the warrant at all tells me that I have to watch my back."

Kevin spoke up, "See Harry, this is what I told you for years, we can't play nice, I learned that on those streets a long time ago. They're either with us or against us, he was never on our side. You should have made a pair of cement shoes for Mr. Big Shot Levine years ago."

Harry turned to him, "Yes and I know you don't like the way I do things, I know that you remember the old days. Well the old days ended and it went off with a bang, the Halloween from Hell was the end of the old days. We have to do things differently, so keep everything going as it was, don't panic. But most of all," he looked at Kevin and back to Sophia, "be very careful who you trust."

Monday is the first day of the trial of Harry Goodrich and he has a long list of charges laid at his feet: illegal gambling, loan sharking, prostitution, drug dealing, illegal firearm sales, money laundering, coercion, conspiracy to commit burglary, and perjury.

Some say people are a product of their environment, that may be the case for Harry Goodrich - after all he is from Covenant City.

Covenant City was founded by very religious people in 1633, trying to create a perfect city, a city that would keep the covenant with God. For decades and decades they tried to be the purest city, with the least tolerance for what they considered "sin." With every round of puritanism, came a round of backlash. Over time the black market of the city changed from selling forbidden books, to alcohol in the 1930s, to obscene tapes, to selling illegal substances and so on. By the mid-twentieth century organized crime in Covenant City was a tradition.

You don't have to be an economist to know what happens when there is a lot of money to be made, illegal or not, others will come in to get some of the pot of gold.

By the beginning of the 21st century the big players were made up of four groups, the Italians, the Russians, the Jamaicans, and the Cubans. If you crossed into their territory, it would cost you.

The lines were drawn, but as time went on all four of them began to push into the other's territory. The Northwest was run by the Cubans, it fell into disarray when the Head of the Family, Hector, fell ill and died. Everyone wanted to take over, but all that internal fighting did was leave them vulnerable for the Russians and the Italians to come in and take over, one street corner at a time. The Russians decided to spend money buying out the Jamaicans, while the Italians spent money on extra weapons and inventory.

What began as a price war and a battle for territory got more heated and turned into a real war. It started with one guy being threatened, then another guy would get assaulted in retaliation, and in retaliation to that another guy was hospitalized, and then someone was killed in retaliation to that. Week after week, month after month it continued to escalate and spill onto the streets. Despite all the public demand for law and order, those things were in short supply in Covenant City.

It was during this time that Harry Goodrich joined the Italians as an administrator, a numbers guy. He was smart, charming, and in one case extremely lucky; he left town for Las Vegas to do research- people thought research was a euphemism for partying. While he was away, both sides were thinking the same thing, dress up in costumes and strike on Halloween. If you were with the Russians or the Italians, you had a target on you. Over 1500 murders including innocent bystanders and police officers took place that day, it became known throughout the country and was dubbed by the media as the Halloween from Hell. Both groups were decimated, most of the top guys in either group were killed. The country mourned, many rolled their eyes, the cynical said, "It's Covenant City, what do you expect?"

However, the 930,000 people who lived there were left to ponder, "What's next?"

On November 10 that year, Harry Goodrich returned, not just with a tan, he was a man with a plan.

The First Day of the Trial

The First Day of the Trial

Harry Goodrich got into his limousine where his lawyer Ms. James was waiting for him. She asked Harry, "How are you doing today?"

Harry seemed a little bit bothered, "I would feel better if I knew who gave them enough information on me to take this to a trial."

Ms. James responded by holding his hand, "Are you worried that we won't win this?"

Harry responded, "I know we will win this, it's just really irritating."

Harry Goodrich walked into court that day, as he walked towards the table the people buzzed, as a confident man in his mid-30s he seemed to have the most amount of energy. He walked in as if his he had no weight on his shoulders, his brown eyes still gleamed. His natural charisma shone through as he sat down next to his defense attorney. The prosecuting attorney sat down at the table to their right, Harry Goodrich looked over at the prosecuting attorney, Harry whispered in the ear of Ms. James, "Remember, we got this; this guy can't lace your boots. I can't wait to send him back to his office with his tail between his legs."

Ms. James had a naturally innocent face as she whispered back, "That's what I want to hear. Your future depends on it."

Harry whispered back, "Our future depends on it."

Ms. James looked back at him slightly confused, when the bailiff's voice rang out and the Judge came out to the bench. "All rise, the Honourable Judge Jennifer Reeves presiding."

Judge Reeves sat down on the bench, her frizzy brown hair and glasses indicated her authority. Judge Reeves quickly scanned the file. "We are here for the case of the state of Vermont vs Harry Goodrich, will the respective attorneys please give their opening statements?"

The district attorney, Mr. Levine, in his grey suit and his matching grey short hair stood up and walked towards the jury and judge. Mr. Levine cleared his throat and began his speech. "Your Honour, members of the jury, we in Covenant City have struggled for many decades with crime. Organized crime committed by parasites who sit in an office pretending to be legitimate businessmen. A parasite that exploits our city's most vulnerable citizens while filling our streets with guns, drugs and low-lives. We have an opportunity to put away one of these parasites - his name is Harry Goodrich. You heard the list of charges, and we have a duty to justice and this community to hold Mr. Goodrich accountable for his actions."

Ms. James stood up in her navy blue pants suit, her innocent bright face and brown hair with subtle blonde streaks were naturally endearing to everyone she met. She began to deliver her opening statement, approaching the jury with confidence. "Ladies and gentlemen, the defendant has done nothing but contribute to the community. Like many of you he has grown up in this community and wants nothing more than to help make Covenant City a better place. Amazingly, in the last five years, crime has plummeted to historic lows, and perhaps the defendant's efforts have been a small piece of this progress. If the defendant was the ruthless crime lord spreading guns, drugs, and low-lives the prosecution portrays him as, that would not be the case.

"Let me sum this up: our district attorney, Mr. Levine, is running for re-election this fall and wants material for his campaign ads. There is also something more troubling occurring, this isn't about justice to society, but a personal vendetta. Our justice system is not a system that should railroad innocent people into jail to make elected officials look good. I hope you will see through this for the publicity stunt and petty attack that it is."

Witness: Angela Jamieson

The first witness was called, and after being sworn in she was introduced by Mr. Levine. Her bleach-blonde hair shone, and with a bright smile, the rest of her face was covered under what seemed like five layers of makeup. Mr. Levine spoke to her as the witness took her seat, "Ms. Angela Jamieson, please state how you know the defendant."

Angela began, "I worked in his brothels for two years, subject to terrible conditions, demeaning work and coercion into having sex with strangers."

Her voice indicated that what was being said sounded rehearsed without the acting ability to cover that fact. Mr. Levine continued, "So he was not only aware of this but he was directly involved?"

Angela responded, "Yes." She went on, "He had this natural charisma, I once overheard him talk a girl who had been dead set against it into doing anal. He was so good at convincing people to do anything for his business."

Mr. Levine went on, "So you were a prostitute, and he was a pimp to you and other women?"

Angela responded, "Absolutely."

Mr. Levine paced to Angela's right, turning to face her again, "Would you mind telling people about the horrible conditions he made you work under?"

Angela began to get a little nervous as she told her story, "He came up to me and told me that if I wanted to have a future I would work for his new system. Rather than letting me work from home or standing on the street, he made me work in his place and he had these people watching us called 'security.'

"He would withhold some of the money I made for 'my future' while I had to check the Johns for any signs of STDs. It was a dangerous environment that I was subjected to."

Mr. Levine asked one more question, "So to sum it up for the court, you were a desperate woman who needed help, and he was doing nothing more than exploiting your body and your life, is that correct?"

"Yes," she responded, with a brief pause as if she had to remember that response.

Mr. Levine turned to Judge Reeves, "No further questions, Your Honour."

Ms. James stood up and approached the bench, "Angela, if the defendant really did these things, if he was so horrible then why didn't you go to the police in the first place? Why did you wait years?"

Angela responded, "Well I didn't know if I was safe until they had him in custody."

Ms. James went back to the table and picked up a file, and handed it to the judge. "Your Honour, that is Angela's police record, which indicates that she was offering a plain clothes police officer sex a few months ago. This proves she was continuing her profession without any possible influence from the defendant. I must also state for the court that her testimony is on the basis of her sentence being reduced. I don't believe this witness is trustworthy for that reason."

The judge looked at Angela with a more skeptical gaze as Ms. James continued, "Also, Your Honour, this woman was enrolled in a community college for hospitality over 3 years ago, during the time when this exploitation supposedly happened, and then was thrown out for failing to uphold her GPA in her third semester."

Ms. James walked towards the jury with her hands clasped in front of her, "Tell me, ladies and gentlemen of the jury, why would a controlling, coercive and demeaning pimp allow a prostitute anywhere near a college classroom let alone let her enroll in classes for over a year? Why would a supposedly controlling pimp let her anywhere near an opportunity to be anything else than a prostitute?"

Ms. James walked back to face Angela, "It sounds to me like your life didn't turn out the way you planned and you needed someone to blame because you can't look in the mirror."

Mr. Levine leapt to his feet, "Objection, badgering the witness!"

Ms. James said, raising her index finger, "One final question Your Honour: if my client was the coercive demeaning pimp that you claim he was, how did you stop working for him without issue?"

Angela's eyes went wide, the proverbial deer in the headlights, the courtroom was so silent you could hear a pin drop. After several seconds of continued silence, Ms. James looked to the judge and stated, "No further questions Your Honour. I think that says it all."

Angela stepped down from the witness stand incredibly conflicted and somewhat upset, as Ms. James had hit a nerve. Harry sat there silently, looking reasonably satisfied with the result.

Witness: Corey Pondrell

The next witness stepped forward; Corey Pondrell was sworn in and he came across as a nervous, skinny man with a buzz cut, who seemed to have a significant amount of anxiety.

Mr. Levine began, "Please tell us how you know the defendant."

Corey began, "I was one of the customers buying meth and heroin, suddenly the dealers say they couldn't sell that stuff anymore. After the Halloween from Hell there was hardly anyone to buy from, I had tried to buy from other people but they barely had any, and they would get caught in no time. One day they'd be there and two days later they were caught. I saw this happen a few times."

Corey continued, "Instead of meth or heroin they offered me some rehab, they promised that I would be given a small supply and I could turn my life around. The only reason I went along was because I was desperate, they told me I would be weaned off and they would get me straight."

He began to tear up as Mr. Levine continued, "What happened then?"

Corey responded, "I was sleeping on friends' couches, a couple days here, a couple days there. I was basically homeless and then when I started their rehab I stayed in some building that looked like a cheap motel. Me and a few other people were paired together doing arts and crafts and playing board games. All those games of scrabble couldn't get my mind off the withdrawal. It was almost two months of pure hell as I got less and less heroin and meth."

Mr. Levine continued, "What happened next?"

Corey began to regain his composure, "Then he and two his buddies walk in and they tell me how I owe $3,000 and I will be working it off."

Mr. Levine asked, "How?"

Corey responded, "He told me I would be working as a dishwasher at a local restaurant, it took me almost a year to pay him back. I was being used, it was awful."

Mr. Levine followed, "One final question, were you helped or were you exploited?"

Corey responded, "It was exploitation, I had nothing but they found a way to drain more than $3,000 out of me."

Mr. Levine turned to the jury, "I hope all of that is crystal clear, the struggle of Mr. Pondrell was suffered by many others who were too scared to come forward."

Mr. Levine turned to Judge Reeves, "No further questions Your Honour."

Mr. Levine sat back down and Ms. James stood up and approached the witness stand, as Corey Pondrell leaned back in his chair.

Ms. James began, "So Mr. Pondrell, if we take your story seriously, you were a nearly homeless drug addict. Even by your own story, the defendant took you in and got you clean, a job, and a place to live. How are you doing now?"

He responded, "I work construction, and part time at an auto parts warehouse. I have been clean for four years and I have a one bedroom apartment, still single."

A mild chuckle spread across the courtroom and a smirk came across Ms. James' face.

She began to walk towards the jury to make her point. She placed her hand on the rail in front of the jurors to bring them into the conversation. "Well, there is a reality show I never saw, one where the dealers take a drug addict and turn his life around."

The courtroom laughed louder, "Not only that, but this supposed drug lord, who our district attorney claimed less than 20 minutes ago was 'filling our streets with guns, drugs and low lives,' stopped providing the worst drugs, including one that is an epidemic across the country. Since when do they do that? If after the Halloween from Hell there was no one else to buy from? I don't think you have to be an expert on organized crime to know that they would have made a killing with a drug monopoly. Mr. Levine would have you believe the defendant is some terrible crime boss, his own witnesses' stories don't make sense."

Ms. James walked back towards the judge, "Dare I say, that if we don't get some real evidence soon, this trial will be a complete waste of everyone's time."

The judge's look spelled out her internal conflict and the jury didn't know what to think either.

Witness: Ethan Sawyer

When this witness stepped forward, the courtroom buzzed, the jurors, the crowd, and judge knew his face well. Mr. Levine began, "Please state your name for the record."

The newest witness, with a bowl cut and anger in his eyes, responded with his name, "Ethan Sawyer."

Mr. Levine continued, "Would you please tell the court your story and how you know the defendant?"

He began, "I was a nobody, another homeless guy who hadn't worked in over a year, then one day a couple guys comes up to me and says they might have a job for me. I knew it couldn't be legit but I didn't care at that point. So the guys introduce me to Mr. Goodrich, and he asks me if I want to change my life for the better. I tell him 'of course' and he tells me about some guys that used to be part of their gang who went off on their own doing really bad stuff... child trafficking."

The courtroom gasped as Ethan continued, "He says that if I cut the alarm which he had scouted and knew where it ran under the lawn. Once I disabled the alarm I had to break into the basement I will find some of their victims. Then I call the cops and get myself arrested because they would have to come into the house if I am turning myself in. I thought he was nuts, next thing I know he turns on his charms and tells me I will be a hero. He tells me that he will have a job waiting for me, he tells me that I will be loved by the people. He painted this picture of glory like they would have statues for me, I can't believe I ever listened to that horse shit!"

Judge Reeves spoke up, "Please maintain a civil tongue, this is a courtroom."

He was becoming more upset as his bitterness had risen, Mr. Levine interjected himself into the conversation, "Please calm down and finish your story Mr. Sawyer."

He took a couple deep breaths, "I still wasn't sure, and he sold me this story about how Nelson Mandela spent 27 years in a South African Prison, he came out a hero because of why he went in and how he survived. I would be greeted as a hero after 6-8 months, absolutely no more than a year in jail for doing the right thing. He got me so worked up and enthusiastic to do this great deed that he talked me into. Next thing I know I am walking onto the guy's property, cutting the cord for the alarm that I was told about. I carefully broke the basement window, I crawled in and soon I saw the children in cages. I was so horrified without a second thought I called the cops and finished the plan. One fake story and plea bargain later I am being shuttled off to jail for six months. I don't think it was until a few weeks in jail when I woke up and realized I had been had. He didn't have a job for me, I was a pawn in his street game."

Mr. Levine turned to the jury, "They say once is a fluke, twice is a coincidence, three times is a pattern. Exploitation of the vulnerable, promising something and getting it with major strings attached or not at all. This is an example of Mr. Goodrich's behaviour as a parasite. Just in case this isn't clear, this is conspiracy to commit burglary and perjury. The trial of Ethan Sawyer was closed with the entirely false details about why he had broken into that home in the first place. He did so with the direction of Mr. Goodrich to lie about the circumstances. Once again lying on the witness stand is called perjury and Mr. Goodrich took this poor and very desperate man making him commit burglary and perjury for his own motives. The freeing of the kidnapped children was an accidental side effect of what are despicable crimes."

Mr. Levine turned to the judge, "No further questions Your Honour."

Mr. Levine gave Harry a mocking smirk as he walked back to his table.

Ms. James made one last look to Harry and he nodded. Ms. James stood up holding a DVD in a case, and put it on the edge of the defense's table. She approached the witness stand, "Mr. Sawyer, let me get this straight. So the defendant told you to break into someone's home so you could discover a far worse crime and rescue children from human trafficking?"

Ethan responded, "He was just getting rid of the competition."

A confused look came over her face, "How is it competition if his group didn't participate in that type of crime?"

He lashed back, "He was getting rid of other crime gangs."

She struggled not to laugh, "A crime fighting crime boss, someone call Hollywood, sounds like a movie."

The crowd chuckled but Judge Reeves quickly interrupted, "Please get to the point Ms. James."

Ms. James continued, "So the defendant talked you into doing this, left you in jail with nothing, and did nothing but make you a patsy?"

He said, "Yes, he used me and threw me away like trash."

Ms. James asked, "Is there anything else you would like to say to the court?"

He responded with resentment "What else is there? He tricked me and threw me away and we need to stop him at all costs!"

Ms. James walked back to the table and picked up the DVD. "That is very interesting because I have footage that says otherwise."

She put the DVD in the player, "This is from the correctional facility where Mr. Sawyer served his sentence."

The footage played, and there was Harry Goodrich sitting at a table when Ethan Sawyer was brought to sit opposite him. They shook hands as Harry began to speak to him. "Hello Mr. Sawyer, I am Harry Goodrich, I read your story in the paper and while I can't condone breaking and entering, I think you did it because you were desperate. However the courage you showed in incriminating yourself to save others is amazing and something that proves you deserve a second chance."

On the footage Ethan seemed confused saying, "Okay."

Harry Goodrich continued, "How are you doing in here?"

Ethan said, "I am doing okay right now, I am worried about what will happen when I get out of here."

Harry Goodrich continued, "Well I can't change your sentence, but what I can do is make sure you have a job. I have a job lined up for you as an assistant for a friend of mine who is a lawyer, with your integrity and a fair shot, I believe that when you get out of here things will get better for you."

Ethan seemed shocked, "Really, you got me a job like that?"

Harry Goodrich continued, "Yes, I have heard over and over again about how when people get out of jail they have nowhere to go except the gutter or back to jail. It's a really sad situation, I can't get jobs for everyone, but I think you deserve better than that."

Ethan responded with shock, "Thank you so much."

Harry Goodrich continued, "Well, listen I am going to leave the card of my friend the lawyer and you will get it as soon as you get out of jail."

Ethan responded, "Thank you so much Mr. Goodrich."

They shook hands, Harry Goodrich continued, "Well I have to get going but you have an opportunity waiting for you. This is a tough time, but it isn't the end, a new beginning is just a few more months away, Ethan. Hang in there, I'm rooting for you."

They shook hands and said farewell, the footage then jumped two weeks ahead and a guard came to the table where Harry Goodrich was sitting and said, "He doesn't want to talk to you."

Harry Goodrich looked very confused, "What? Why, did he give a reason?"

The guard went on, "He was saying stuff about you ditching him and using him."

Harry Goodrich looked absolutely baffled by what he was being told, "I guess I will come back later, could you please talk to him and try to find out what is going on. I am simply trying to give him a second chance at life."

The guard shrugged his shoulders, "I don't know what to tell you. I mean if I was in his shoes I would be glad I had something and someone waiting for me when I get out."

Harry and the guard shook hands and Harry left shaking his head.

The footage skipped forward three more weeks showing the same type of situation. The guard once again said that Ethan Sawyer didn't want to talk to him and was saying stuff about how he had been tricked and was being treated like a pawn. Harry Goodrich once again left saying that he hoped that Ethan Sawyer would change his mind.

The footage skipped another five weeks and showed Harry Goodrich along with another man who he identified as his lawyer Mr. Brooks who Ethan could be working for once he got out of jail. They waited and waited and Ethan had refused to come out.

The guard shook his head saying, "Look Mr. Goodrich, I don't know what is going on in his head, I don't know whether the guys in the jail are telling him stuff to make him paranoid. I don't know but the fact is I don't think he is going to change his mind, we'll give him the card that you left at your first visit. As sad as it is I think that you are just wasting your time."

Harry and Mr. Brooks shook the guard's hand and they left with Harry's head looking down at the ground overcome with disappointment.

The guard seeing his expression added, "Mr. Goodrich, don't feel bad, you're doing what you can but you can't help those who won't help themselves."

Before leaving the room Harry responded with an obligatory, "Thank you."

The footage stopped as Ms. James turned towards the jury after picking up a piece of paper. "Mr. Sawyer, despite the passionate story you told, that doesn't sound like abandoning a patsy, especially given his persistence."

Ms. James walked up to Judge Reeves, "Your Honour this is a bill he received from Mr. Brooks' firm for the last day on the tape, charging the defendant $810.00 for 135 minutes of his time."

She handed the bill to the judge who looked at it and then turned to Ethan Sawyer, "Are there any other details you forgot to mention in your testimony that you want to say?"

Ethan began to look absolutely overwhelmed as if his reality itself was coming apart, "That is impossible – he rigged that tape, he wasn't really there, there was no job being offered. I was screwed!"

He stood up furiously looking right at Harry Goodrich pointing at him in an enraged manner, "You are the devil himself!"

Harry looked at him with shock and disbelief as Ethan started yelling at everyone else, "Are you blind? He is the devil, he doctored that footage! Can't you see that?"

The judge spoke up, "Mr. Sawyer, calm down, that footage came directly from the jail you were kept at and never left the property of either the jail or the evidence locker. Now please get control of yourself Mr. Sawyer."

He leapt up trying to attack the judge yelling, "He is the lord of lies, you are one of his disciples."

The Bailiff and other security immediately pulled him off of Judge Reeves. Judge Reeves declared that he was in contempt of court and that he be removed. Mr. Levine had his face in his hand due to the disastrous end result of his witness' testimony.

The Judge banged her gavel, "I am declaring a brief recess, we will get to the final round of witnesses today."

Just as the people began to make their way to the exits Mr. Levine came over to Harry Goodrich and Ms. James, "You got lucky right there, but you can't hide for too much longer. Mark my words you are going to prison for a long time."

Ms. James responded, "Instead of worrying about us, I think you should be worried about your witness' anger management."

Mr. Levine stepped away as Ms. James turned to Harry Goodrich, "Well, so far so good."

Witness: Walter Evans

They came back from recess and Harry Goodrich's first witness entered the witness stand and was sworn in. Walter Evans was a black man who had hair that was almost two inches high, with determination he sat in the witness stand.

Ms. James approached, "Please state your name for the record."

He responded, "My name is Walter Evans."

She continued, "Would you mind telling us how you know Mr. Goodrich?"

He responded, "I came here to defend him because four years ago I was accused of armed robbery, but I didn't do it. Hell I was visiting my wife's family in Illinois when that happened. I tried to talk to the public defender, but he didn't give a damn. He just spent an hour trying to sell me on giving in and taking a plea bargain which would have included a criminal record. That would be the end of my ability to vote and something that may have destroyed me financially because people don't hire convicts, and a black convict, forget it."

The crowd was split between discomfort and mild laughter.

Ms. James asked, "So when did you meet Mr. Goodrich?"

Walter responded, "I told my friend about what was going on and he told me about his friend who was in a similar situation. I was reluctant, but I didn't have many options, so I told him to get me his contact information."

Ms. James continued, "So you reached out to him thinking he could help you out of your bad situation."

Walter responded, "Absolutely."

Ms. James continued, "What exactly did the defendant say to you?"

Walter took a hard look at Mr. Levine, "Harry Goodrich told me exactly what was going to happen, he said that the public defenders either don't give a damn or don't give enough time and they will start pressuring me into signing my life away. Sure enough three days later I had that meeting where they tried to do exactly that all over again. I told them they weren't selling me down the river, but they didn't care how much evidence or what would happen to me."

There was another awkward silence, as Ms. James cleared her throat, "So the public defender didn't even attempt to give you a real defence in your case?"

Walter became upset, "Damn right they didn't, they didn't care that I didn't do it. They didn't care that I had kids who needed me, they were just ready to toss me in a cell. Mr. Goodrich told me he would loan me the extra money I would need, and gave me a good attorney and I was acquitted. If it weren't for Mr. Goodrich, my life would have been ruined."

Walter gave a harsh scowl to Mr. Levine who directed his own scowl towards Harry Goodrich. Ms. James looked up to Judge Reeves, "No further questions Your Honour."

Mr. Levine stood up and approached the bench, "Mr. Evans, I need to ask you a couple of questions. First, how do we know that he isn't threatening you into this testimony today, he was very intimidating to the other witnesses I brought here."

Walter was staring a hole through him, "I don't care what the rest of those jive witnesses say, that man there saved my life. I can only imagine how many people weren't so lucky who were just thrown away like garbage because that's all you think black people are you son of a bitch."

Judge Reeves immediately banged her gavel, "Mr. Evans, this is a court of law, please answer the questions and watch your language."

He looked up at Judge Reeves, irritated, "To answer your question, he didn't threaten me, he didn't pay me, I'm here because he deserves his freedom just like I do, end of story."

A few people in the audience began to applaud, when Judge Reeves banged her gavel and called for silence.

Mr. Levine said, "I would like to ask this witness one final question. Mr. Evans, you mentioned a loan, what was the interest rate he asked from you?"

Walter responded, "I don't remember the rate, but I remember it was cheaper than those cheque cashing places and you let them run around free."

Mr. Levine insisted, "Are you evading the question, Mr. Evans?"

Walter looked at him with complete disdain, "No I actually don't remember, when you are fighting for your freedom, some percentage figure doesn't mean a damn thing."

He responded, "So you could have been a victim of loan sharking depending on the terms, he could have taken advantage of you in your moment of desperation."

Walter scoffed, "My moment of desperation yes, that you and your office put me into in the first place. He saved me, I've had so many wonderful moments with my kids these last few years because of him, something you and your office were happy to tear away from me."

Mr. Levine looked out of the corner of his eye, he could see the jurors looking at him with concern or disgust. Trying not to show his frustration, Mr. Levine turned to Judge Reeves, "No further questions Your Honour."

He went back to his chair as Judge Reeves told Walter he could step down. Walter nodded at Harry and Ms. James as he walked towards the second last row of the seats where he gave his wife a big hug. Harry looked back with a brief smile coming to his face hearing Walter say, "You were great baby."

Witness: Bill Moretti

Ms. James called her next witness to the stand, she scanned the faces of the jury hoping to tell where they stood. The witness was a seventy year old man with thinning grey hair, and small glasses.

Ms. James began, "Would you please state your name for the record?"

He responded, "My name is Bill Moretti, a lot of people just call me 'Willy.'"

Ms. James went on, "Would you please tell the court what you do and how you know Mr. Goodrich?"

Bill went on, "Well, I've been the owner of ice cream trucks for years and years, I owned four trucks, and had a few employees driving them around. Unfortunately, it's getting harder and harder to do that when you have to compete with the chains. You can only run several months of the year, and with the weather getting more volatile it cuts our season even shorter. Not to mention, at my age it gets harder and harder to afford health insurance for myself, my wife, and even for my employees."

Ms. James pushed, "So how do you know Mr. Goodrich?"

Bill responded, "He actually helped me a lot, he said he was willing to buy the business from me but still keep me and my employees on. I actually make more money now as one of his employees than I did as the owner of our operation."

Ms. James asked, "How would you describe Mr. Goodrich to the courtroom?"

Bill continued, "He struck me as a very sentimental person, how he heard about my business I don't know, but he made me an offer and he's taken a lot of concerns off my plate. He's been great to work for and I think he wants Covenant City to be a safe place. He's lived here his whole life and he once told me about how one time when he was a teenager he had seen an ice cream truck like mine that had been attacked and robbed. He told me he could still remember seeing the designs on the side of the truck with bullet holes in it and he was just heartbroken by it. His goal is to make this city a better place."

Ms. James continued, "So why did he tell you he was buying your business?"

Bill responded, "He said he wanted to make it a nice place to live and the ice cream business is one of those things that adds a nice touch to neighbourhoods and makes a street a nicer place."

Ms. James thanked him, and said, "No further questions Your Honour."

Mr. Levine stepped forward, with sarcasm in his voice, "Your Honour, as nice and as wonderful as all of that sounds, let's not kid ourselves here: Mr. Goodrich isn't some Mr. Rogers sentimentalist, he bought a struggling business for one reason – cash. Money Laundering 101 says you use cash based businesses, especially ones without receipts, and you run those to send your illegal money through them. The fact that he is using these operations that are literally driving through our neighbourhoods to funnel his filthy money should sicken us all."

Mr. Levine turned to the jury, "If any of you are still doubtful of Mr. Goodrich's real intentions, he also runs strip clubs, does that make Covenant City a nice bright, family friendly place to live?"

Judge Reeves interrupted, "Mr. Levine do you have any questions for Mr. Moretti?"

Mr. Levine turned back towards them, "I was just getting to those Your Honour. Mr. Moretti, if you were struggling how could he afford to keep the enterprise going for the last few years?"

Bill responded, "I sold him the business, I never saw the financials after that and I was glad to not have to worry about that anymore."

Mr. Levine was completely unsatisfied, "Mr. Moretti, my other question was this, didn't you think it was odd that a man who runs strip clubs, which is a business clearly aimed at adults, would expand into an industry that is the exact opposite? What does that have in common with ice cream trucks?"

Bill leaned forward in his chair, "I once asked him, why are you doing that?"

Mr. Levine motioned for more answers. "His response really struck me, he said 'besides market diversification' he said, 'we have cured and treated a lot of diseases but the one that is infecting everyone is stress. A world where your problems follow you, where you can't just have a bad day and wake up the next day and leave it behind you. Everything is more complicated which means whatever happened the previous day follows you.'

"So he said that these two industries do something wonderful, a kid who may be having a terrible day, who may be having a bad time at home can suddenly hear music and for a few minutes they can be a kid without a care in the world.

"As for the other industry, some guys who could have any number of problems, who feel like they don't matter, who seem to just be an easily replaceable part in their corporation's machine, can go somewhere for an evening. All of that can disappear and they can be treated like they matter, for a brief period they don't have to be invisible."

There was an odd silence that spread across the courtroom, "In that small way they are very similar and I think he feels a lot of empathy for the average person struggling to make it through life."

Mr. Levine looked over at the jury, fearing he was losing them to this sympathetic older man. He said, "No further questions, Your Honour."

Witness: Dinesh Chopra

Mr. Levine called his next witness, hoping to gain back some of the ground he had lost. His witness was Mr. Dinesh Chopra, a middle aged, clean-shaven man, who was balding leaving only darker grey hair coming out of the back and sides of his head.

Mr. Levine began, "Please state your name for the record."

Dinesh leaned forward, "Dinesh Chopra."

Mr. Levine continued with a renewed confidence. "Would you please state how you know Mr. Goodrich?"

Dinesh responded, "I am the owner of two stores, a convenience store first, and then I bought the dry cleaning business next door seven or eight years ago. During all of that time toiling night and day to build a life for my family, thugs would threaten me and tell me that I needed to pay protection money or else. If it had just been a couple of punks I would have just told them to jump off a cliff, but there were six of them. They were armed and other people in the area, including Mr. Chow the owner of a Chinese food place down the road, told me I had do it or my family would be in danger. For over ten years I paid those thugs every month, every once in a while they would raise the cost on me, if my store wasn't so popular and if I wasn't so good with my money I might not have survived."

Mr. Levine let out a sigh of disappointment, "Mr. Chopra, please tell the court how you know Mr. Goodrich."

Ms. James was taking notes while Mr. Chopra replied, "One day, about three months after the Halloween from Hell, a few guys come up to me at the front of my store and tell me I owe for my protection money for the last two months, I almost leapt over the counter to strangle them. Just before I could seriously consider it, they write down an address and say 'Go to this address and you won't have to pay it anymore.' Let me tell you, you have to sell a lot of bottles of pop, a lot of candy bars, and dry clean a lot of clothes to save $1100 a month, so I went. That was when I met that man."

A mild buzz spread over the courtroom as Dinesh pointed at Harry and then continued, "He tells me that he is 'the new boss and they

The Great Gangster

don't do things that way anymore. After all, charging protection money drains money from the community.' I told him 'Damn right it does.' So he tells me that instead of paying $1100 a month the new deal is that I just have to hire one person full time at $15 an hour. The person in question owes them money, if I have to fire him I am allowed to as long as I tell them why and replace them with some other person who owes them.

"I objected, I'm no fool, I would be paying $600 a week, four weeks a month that is $2,400 a month I would be paying double. Then Mr. Goodrich tells me 'You're looking at this all wrong, you aren't just paying double, you are gaining a tax write-off, you are losing an expense and gaining a loyal employee. If they aren't, you can fire them until we find the right fit. Besides, running two stores is a lot of work, think about it this way, we are helping the local economy, you can take it easier because this person can take over whatever needs to be done.' I suddenly remembered who I was talking to, a low life crime boss. I reluctantly accepted, even though the person they sent me was hard working, I couldn't help but wonder how afraid he was of being fired by me. I am trying to save for college for my children, I want to throw these dirt bags like him in prison."

Mr. Levine's face was once again very confident, "So Dinesh, were there any threats or any other harassment that occurred?"

Dinesh responded, "Nothing obvious, because I didn't want to provoke these thugs."

Mr. Levine turned to the jury, "So, an immigrant comes to this country, works hard all of his life, trying to give the American Dream to his family," Mr. Levine let out a resigned sigh, before continuing, "only for this parasite, Mr. Goodrich, to use him to leech money from him going to other vulnerable people. As you just heard, the buck stops there and goes into his pocket."

The courtroom chuckled another time. "Once again exploitation of economically vulnerable people, like I said before, three times is a pattern and we are now up to four times."

Mr. Levine then turned to Judge Reeves, "No more questions Your Honour."

Ms. James stood up, quickly scanning the jury who appeared to have been moved by Mr. Chopra's statements. She approached the bench with focus, and finally put her hand on the rail of the witness bench. "Mr. Chopra, I have a few questions, the first one is if this had been going on for well over fifteen years why are you only coming forward now?"

Dinesh replied, "I had to make sure that I would be safe. I have been threatened by thugs before."

A confused look came over Ms. James' face, "There was no threat to you for years and yet you still lived in such fear?"

He responded, "Yes, I have to watch out for my family."

She paused, "I have another very important question for you Mr. Chopra: this employee who they supposedly made you hire, what is the status of the debt he is supposedly using your job to pay off?"

Dinesh shrugged saying, "I don't know, it was the one subject we didn't talk about after the first day. We just work together to get through our unfortunate circumstances."

The confusion on the face of Ms. James became even greater. "So let me get this straight, you have had this employee for almost five years against your will, the reason why is his debt that he supposedly owed the defendant and you have no idea whether or not the loan is paid off? That means that according to your story, this 'low life crime boss' as Mr. Levine keeps calling him, may not be getting anything anymore and stopped collecting money possibly years ago. Mr. Chopra, you are an entrepreneur, a business man, tell me, why would any business man with two revenue streams eliminate the permanent one and keep the one that is supposed to be temporary?"

Dinesh's confusion came to the surface, "I don't know how bad men think."

She paused and said, "So you have no explanation for this stark contradiction in your own story?"

The judge looked at him with a contemplative look on her face, seriously considering everything she had heard in the last few minutes. Ms. James continued after turning to face the jury, "The only thing the district attorney has said that is correct is that three times is a pattern and we are now at four. The difference is, the pattern are stories that make no sense, and in the case of the previous testimony, willfully dismissing facts in an attempt to make them fit an irrational narrative."

Ms. James turned one more time to Dinesh, "Are there any other details or things you want to add to your story? Anything you may have just remembered right now?"

Dinesh paused and said, "A crime is a crime, no matter how weird it is."

Ms. James paused, "Well, in order to determine if a crime happened, we have to know if the story makes sense. You can tell me about a crime, but if your story includes rain coming off the ground and going into the sky, people will have a hard time believing you, and with good reason."

Ms. James turned back to Judge Reeves, "I have no more questions

Your Honour."

Judge Reeves announced , "Mr. Chopra, you may step down. We are just about at our time for the day. This trial will resume a week from this upcoming Wednesday, and on a quick note, I fully intend to press charges against Mr. Sawyer, for his attempted assault on me as it is apparent that he needs psychological help. Finally to the prosecution, please screen your witnesses more carefully so we can avoid ugly incidents like the one we saw earlier today. That will be all."

Judge Reeves banged her gavel, as the court stood up and began to exit. Mr. Levine began to put his files in his bag with frustration, as if he felt like he was losing already. Anyone within five feet of him could hear his grumbling and he walked out with an angry stride.

This was not lost on Harry Goodrich, who said to Ms. James, "I'm guessing that he spent so much time studying the law that his friends never taught him how to use a poker face."

Between the First and Second Day of the Trial

Between the First and Second Day of the Trial

Harry Goodrich had already won his bail hearing several weeks ago, so he was going home. He was leaving the courtroom, bracing himself for the barrage because the media was waiting outside the courtroom. Ms. James stated to them as they walked through the crowd, "Mr. Goodrich has nothing to say at this time."

The flashes of the cameras and the obstruction of people with microphones almost made it impossible for Mr. Goodrich to get to the limousine that was waiting for him. Finally, as he got in, his assistant Brian opened up the mini bar in the back, "What do you feel like having, Harry?"

Harry, with his hand over the ridge of his jaw said, "Rum and orange juice."

As the drink began to be made, Harry asked Ms. James, "What do you think his strategy will be next Wednesday?"

She responded, "Well, he will definitely need to work on the coherence of the witnesses' stories, and he will need stronger evidence of the supposed exploitation, so we will have to prepare for that. He's already in a hole, Ethan Sawyer's breakdown on the stand really damaged him."

Harry waited a moment as he peered out the window, Brian said, "Harry."

Harry looked to Brian who was handing him his drink and he looked out the window again after taking a gulp. "I'm sorry, my fault, I asked you an incomplete question. The question I should have asked is, what do you think his strategy will be next Wednesday, given that he is being driven by a personal grudge rather than any of the normal reasons that drives a prosecutor to pursue a case?"

Ms. James asked, "What makes you say that?"

Harry responded, "Normally if they go after an organized crime ring they go after as many as possible hoping for one of two scenarios: number one, they hope that the lesser guys will rat out the top guys. Scenario number two, if they can't get the guys on top, they can take away some of the underlings, weakening his group a lot. He is only going after me, which confirms to me that this isn't just political – it's personal."

Ms. James continued, "I'm not sure, honestly there wasn't a course in law school called 'how to win personal grudge cases.'"

They both let out a laugh as Ms. James continued, "Well, whichever way he goes, I think we are off to a good start."

Every day Harry would read the newspaper, specifically the articles about his trial. The articles in the paper speculated and it seemed like the editorials and articles were getting more and more outrageous in their opinions.

Brian, after a few days of seeing him do this, asked him, "Why do you keep reading those stories, shouldn't you get away from it for a while? If I had to think about that all the time, it would drive me nuts."

Harry looked up from the newspaper and folded it to put it down on the table. "Brian, this trial is very serious and I can't read the minds of the jurors, but I might be able to get some insight into what they might be thinking by examining the court of public opinion."

Brian paused, "So what is the public saying?"

Harry responded, "The articles seem to be split between two sentiments, the first one is that the district attorney is doing this trial to make himself look like he is doing more than he is. The other articles are saying that they have to crush me before I bring the city back to the way things were five years ago."

Brian began to laugh, "I guess nobody told them that isn't part of the plan?"

Harry laughed as well, "I know, the twelve steppers say the definition of insanity is doing the same thing over and over and expecting a different result. I was lucky not to be there when the Halloween from Hell happened. A lot of people died, nobody won and everybody suffered. I am not putting me or anyone else through that again."

Brian finally asked, "I have been wanting to ask this for a while, but if they do put you in jail, who takes over?"

Harry responded, "It's nothing personal, I'm just too paranoid to tell anyone what the plan is."

Brian said, "Come on, you can trust me, I'm on your side and have been ever since you took over."

Harry responded, "I have been very careful, so the fact that someone gave Levine some of our information including former clients and workers tells me that someone isn't loyal."

Brian asked, "Who do you think it is?"

Harry paused, "I don't know, hopefully the trial will shut it down, but whoever it is might try something else. Besides, if I name a succes-

The Great Gangster

sor it would be a secret because I wouldn't want the successor to have a target on them."

Brian seemed disappointed by the lack of an answer but conceded, "I guess you're right, it's a dangerous time."

The day before the trial, Sophia called, "Hey Harry, tell me, are you ready for the trial, what's the plan?"

Harry paused and said, "Well my lawyer is going to explain it to me later today but what I can say is that I fully intend to push the fact that crime is going down. This isn't five or ten years ago, not everyone is a crime boss anymore, I'll play the 'he's paranoid' card."

Sophia paused, "Well if the worst happens I promise I will do the best I can with whoever is in charge."

Harry said, "Don't worry, I'm sure you will."

After Harry hung up the phone he paused, thinking to himself, "I hope I am trusting the right people. I know the city has struggled, I don't want to go back to the old days, no sane person does. I also don't want Mr. Levine to just run things how he wants, I can't let him win."

The day before the second day of the trial, Harry Goodrich was sitting in his office typing up a new proposal, with the local news playing in the background.

Suddenly, the newscasters shifted topics. "Now on to legal news, there is a tremendous amount of speculation regarding the Harry Goodrich trial. While no direct footage of the trial was taken, the topics of the testimony have spread like wildfire. Harry Goodrich has gone from being a barely known businessman to being one of the most controversial figures in the city's recent history. With the second day of the trial happening tomorrow we asked some of the local citizens their thoughts."

The camera footage cut to random people on the street, the first one, a man appearing to be in his forties with a long thick beard and glasses. "I think this is fake, everyone knows the D. A. wants to make it look like he is doing everything but he has done nothing."

The next person was an older woman who looked to be in her sixties, her face was full of concern, "I am so glad that they are tackling this now, before it gets any more out of hand. We have to trap these cockroaches before they spread across our city again."

Another young woman, probably in her twenties responded, "I think that instead of going after people like this we need to do more to stop these mass shooters. When are we going to do something about that?"

Another young man in his twenties responded, "I am so tired of living in one of the worst cities in the country, I hate these criminals that make our city a punchline. I wish we could give every single one of them the death penalty."

The newscasters then mentioned, "We also decided to bring on our legal expert Jim Costello to give us some more insight into the case."

Harry moved to the edge of his seat because he knew this person, this person was one of his lawyers that he had worked with several times before.

Jim began, "The first day of the court battle was quantity versus quality, the prosecution brought more people to testify, but Mr. Goodrich's attorney did an excellent job tearing them down. This is criminal defence 101, when you have anyone testifying against you, you question their credibility. You tear them down and you build your own counter-message, his addition of his own witnesses helped him a lot."

The newscaster asked, "So do you think Mr. Goodrich will be found innocent?"

His response was, "I think that the numbers may eventually catch up with him but he might just be able to give the jurors enough reasonable doubt."

Harry turned off the TV, he immediately called Sophia, "Hey Sophia, were you watching the news?"

She seemed puzzled, "Which one?"

Harry responded, "Channel 245, when was the last time you spoke to Costello?"

Sophia responded, "Our last case involving him wrapped up over four months ago. I offered him two more cases since then but he said he was too busy."

Harry paused, "Don't offer him anything else, if he asks you any questions, don't tell him anything. He seems to have switched his allegiance. Also don't tell a soul about this conversation."

Sophia responded with concern, "Okay, Harry."

Harry paused again, "If you hear anything from Costello, make sure you let me know."

Harry asked Alicia to come into the office. She obliged and he asked, "Are all of our files still in the storage lockers in Providence?"

She said, "Yes, they have been ever since we got them out the night of the arrest."

He continued, "Let me know about any and all phone calls coming in and out of this office, the exact time and no matter how frivolous the call."

The Second Day of the Trial

The Second Day of the Trial

Kevin called Harry about an hour before he was going in for the second day of the trial. He asked him if he was ready, Harry said it was fine and he felt confident. Kevin began to ask slightly probing questions about what his strategy was, Harry paused, "Why are you so interested, are you planning to be a lawyer?"

Kevin began to say "No I am just worried, I don't want anything to happen to you. You can't trust some people like that no good Costello, I'd be happy to make that backstabber disappear."

Harry responded, "I am being very careful, we aren't magicians so no one is disappearing, I can handle Levine. I will walk out of that court with no problems."

Kevin responded, "Well, if you need me to deal with Costello or Levine the old fashion way, I would be happy to. I miss the old days, it was a lot simpler."

Harry said, "Well don't even think about it, we don't do things that way anymore. Talk to you later and take off your nostalgia goggles while you're at it."

The phone call ended with Harry pausing, wondering what the real purpose of the phone call was.

Everyone rose for Judge Jennifer Reeves who sat down on the bench. She asked if anyone had any statements before the first witness of the day was called. Mr. Levine stood up and said, "Yes Your Honour."

Mr. Levine walked over to the jurors, "This man would have you believe that he is innocent and that he should return to our streets. The defence recently cited our city's downturn in crime as if he isn't part of the problem and he might even help. As easy as that sounds remember, people like Mr. Goodrich are a disease on this city, we have to stomp it out now before it is too late and his thugs wipe out all the progress we have made. I hope that the testimony you hear today will remove any and all doubt of Mr. Goodrich's guilt and the threat he poses to Covenant City."

Mr. Levine resumed his seat and Judge Reeves addressed Ms. James, "Your opening statement?"

Ms. James stood up and walked over to the jurors. "Ladies and gentlemen of the jury, during the first day of the trial we had ridiculous story after ridiculous story, apparently some more may be on their way. With any luck today will make it extremely clear that these charges are unfounded and without merit so that we can declare Mr. Goodrich innocent and move on with our lives. Thank you all very much."

Witness: Boris Lebedev

Mr. Levine called his witness, Boris Lebedev to the stand, he was an overweight 36 year old man who was shaved bald and had a scruffy beard that appeared to be starting to turn grey at the very edges of the whiskers. As he took the stand and was sworn in Harry rolled his eyes, not taking his swearing to tell the truth seriously.

Mr. Levine walked to the witness stand and asked, "Boris, would you please begin by telling the court how you know Mr. Goodrich, when you and he met, and your relationship with him from that point?"

Boris began, "That Halloween was awful, so many people died, my own family members. I went to so many funerals in the days and weeks that followed that I became numb, that was the hardest time of my life."

Mr. Levine went on to ask, "Were you involved in the criminal activity of the Russian mob?"

Boris reluctantly said "Yes, I was one of their bookies, I did a lot of research keeping on top of the sports world, issuing odds all of that."

The district attorney paused, "So you were part of their operations and suffered terribly in the Halloween from Hell?"

Boris, in a resigned voice, said, "Yes," while nodding.

Ms. James began taking notes as Mr. Levine's questioning continued, "So when did you first get into contact with Harry, and what was your relationship with him afterwards?"

Boris began, "It was December, I get a phone call from my cousin who told me he was getting out of the business, he had been shot in the spine and could barely move. He told me he had gotten a phone call from someone on the Italian's side who was trying to recruit and told me to get out while I still could. I took the phone call anyway and I was asked about speaking to the guy who was becoming the new boss. I didn't know what was going to happen so I came armed with a few guns and a small knife just in case. We met at the agreed upon address and they frisked me and found my guns, but they missed my small knife. I had to hope that this wasn't a trap, I just didn't know what to do with my future."

Mr. Levine asked, "So what did he offer you?"

Boris continued, "He asked me how I was doing, I told him I was a little concerned, he chuckled and started his sales pitch. 'Exactly,' Goodrich said, 'we were the enemy, everyone was scared, everyone was territorial and we've both been to so many funerals it seems like everybody is dead.'

"He sat down looking me right in the face, 'We both have been through too much and it is time to change things. I want to rebuild and I want you to take all the gambling addicts you have on your Rolodex and offer to help them with their finances and instead of us making money on their loss, let's give them tips on who will win and take a piece of the action.'

"I was very confused and I asked 'What do you mean help them with their finances?' He responded 'Many of the people we make money off of are gambling addicts who are driving their lives into a ditch. If we can help them turn it around we can make a lot of little sustainable bits rather than creating a bunch more desperate people.' I was confused 'If they are desperate and they need us, this city is full of people that need and want us, this city is a great big pot of gold.'

"He responded, 'Yes it is, and with every great big pot of gold are a bunch of people coming to get some. I would rather have a smaller pot of gold, that is containable and requires minimal maintenance, than a great big one that has piles of bodies lying around it.' So he told me what he wanted to re-assign me to and I went home to think about it, I mean agreeing to work for the Italians would have been high treason just a few months earlier, but now they weren't even Italian anymore, this guy was as Italian as supermarket frozen pizza."

The people in the courtroom laughed as Mr. Levine let out a mild chuckle before continuing, "So did you agree to this?"

Boris responded, "Yes, and it gave me the biggest headache imaginable. I had people telling me they wanted to bet on a local fight and I was supposed to ask them about how they were doing financially. I got better at it but I lost a few people early on, suddenly I was supposed to be a bookie, who tells them who to bet on and then we get a piece of their profits and I was supposed to help people who were struggling sort out their finances like those debt people on TV. You would be amazed how much money people would save if they didn't go out for dinner three to five times a week or order stupid stuff online."

More laughs came across the courtroom, Mr. Levine continued, "So, what you are telling us Boris, is that this man hired a bookie to tell people how to manage their finances and how to gamble differently so

The Great Gangster

that they would win far more than they lose?"

Boris responded, "Yes, I was right about 90% of the time on anything local and 60-70% on anything else, and he was always telling me to tell them to treat these bets like investments, bet on a bunch of things so that if you bet on one that doesn't work it doesn't kill you."

Mr. Levine continued, "Ninety percent, that is incredible – would you mind telling the court how you were so good?"

He responded, "I studied very carefully and usually I could figure out the pros and cons of one side winning over the other. Even then, I knew they were up to something when they told me to send all my predictions to them before I send them to the clients. So I have a feeling that they probably put their hands on the scales to help make sure we won way more than we lost. I heard him say a few times, 'Winning clients were repeat clients.'"

There was a murmur across the courtroom as Mr. Levine turned to the judge, "No further questions Your Honour."

Ms. James approached the bench with seemingly no pressure on her shoulders. "Let me get this straight, so you were an organized criminal who was part of a gang that was slaughtered. So you agreed to continue committing illegal behaviour for a different crime group, additionally you are saying that you were offering to help people sort out their finances. Furthermore, if you are getting your clients to, as you put it, all vote the same way, who were you collecting money from?"

Boris responded, "From the non-customers, we actually bankrupted a fledgling numbers bookie gang before. We did it a couple times so that we could avoid it."

Ms. James continued, "How long were you doing this job?"

Boris responded, "Three years."

Her eyes lit up, "Three years, in all of that time, you must have had an incredible amount of back and forth correspondence. With all of these predictions so that they could rig all of these races, fights and whatever else these people were betting on?"

Boris continued, "None, everything was done hard copy and he shredded everything, he was paranoid."

Her eyes rolled, "So, you were working full time predicting things to bet on and you have no paper trail? Do you even have bills from couriers? Don't you have the bills that would show you shipping things regularly to some place the defendant is associated with?"

He said, "No, his people always picked it up several times a week and they were very discreet."

Her eyes became very wide as she turned to the jury, "So, ladies and gentlemen of the jury, this man claims that he had to send papers off every day, that is inefficient to say the least. At this point this should be obvious, how many thousand people is he employing in order to get people to drive to wherever you were working and then drive it to his office then they would send more people to rig everything? This man is not the head of the CIA, not to mention, we have all of these simpler ways of doing things like this. You have offered nothing in terms of phone records, wouldn't common sense say use e-mails?"

The crowd chuckled as Mr. Levine began to bristle, looking around fearing that he was losing his momentum.

Ms. James turned to the judge, "Your Honour, this sounds suspicious to say the least, doesn't it sound odd that he worked with this person for 3 years and has no evidence, just this vague story. We don't even know why he stopped working at what he was doing or for that matter what he is doing now."

Boris spoke up, "I quit because I was tired of making all of these little bits of money and not making the money we used to."

The eyes of Mr. Levine flared up as Ms. James said with a deep accusation in her voice, "So what did you do? Commit other crimes? Loan sharking?"

Boris stood up, losing all composure, "I did until one of his guys ratted me out, as if I didn't know that he was trying to eliminate the competition, you put me behind bars for 12 months you son of a bitch!"

An almost devious smile came across the face of Harry, Ms. James once again turned to the judge, "Your Honour, I think it should be obvious that this witness cannot be trusted to be objective. He clearly has some personal vendetta against my client and he may have committed perjury while on the witness stand today."

Ms. James turned away, looking at Harry Goodrich and pausing for a moment. She turned again to face the jury, "Even if this man is being completely honest, my client is trying to help people. He took old fashioned cut throat bookies off the streets, wow, we have gone from mass violence in the streets to the criminals calling the cops on each other? Do I even have to tell you that it doesn't match with the district attorney's statement from the first day of this trial that he is the second coming of the gangs that ran loose in our streets for years? People of the jury, I think it should be fairly obvious that our district attorney Mr. Levine once again is wasting our time telling us stories that don't make sense. Perhaps even more disturbing, he seems to be aligning himself with actual criminals in the process. I hope this makes it clear that this is not about justice, this is something else that has no place in a court room."

Judge Jennifer Reeves interrupted, "Do you have any more questions for Mr. Lebedev? If not can we move on?"

Ms. James responded, "No further questions your Honour."

Boris Lebedev got off the stand with Harry Goodrich looking at him and shaking his head in disappointment.

Witness: Rico Palumbo

Mr. Levine called his next witness to the stand, Rico Palumbo. Rico's slicked back hair and fine suit made him appear very confident. After being sworn in he started asking questions, "Would you mind telling the court how you know Mr. Goodrich?"

Rico responded, "I ran the gun library, you could either buy a gun or rent a gun, we did both."

Mr. Levine asked, "Could you clarify what you mean by renting a gun and what that entailed?"

He went on to say, "The original game was this, if you had somebody that you wanted to kill, intimidate, threaten, whatever, you rent a gun from us for 24 hours, 48 hours, the longest we ever did was five days. We don't ask any questions, you do whatever it is, you give it back to us. If the cops came looking for it, they wouldn't find it on the guy and if they ever found the gun we had a guy who split his time between growing weed in his basement and cleaning any prints and DNA off the guns."

The jury murmured, as Mr. Levine continued, "So was Mr. Goodrich aware of your actions?"

Rico responded, "I don't know when he found out, but I'm sure he knew that our operations included it. As soon as he took over, he tried to shut us down. I objected at first but he kept saying that we were changing things and this wasn't part of the way we were going to keep doing things. He shut down the whole thing, completely changed that whole game, I had a few guys asking me for guns and I told them we don't do that anymore."

Mr. Levine asked, "How did he do that, did he call the police?"

Rico responded, "No, he came up with a whole different game, he told me to leave town with all the guns and to sell them cheap to small time gun stores in rural towns out west. Places like North and South Dakota, Nebraska, Montana, places like that."

Mr. Levine nodded his head in agreement obviously knowing this story before. "So he takes over the gang and sends you out of the state to do illegal weapons transactions, far away rather than in the city. That

The Great Gangster

is very interesting, I would like to ask you another question, did he tell you why he was doing this?"

Rico responded, "I asked him that same question because we had a good racket going on, even a handful of regular customers and what he said to me was that you are a lot more likely to get caught red handed when you spill blood. He was full of weird sayings like that, he also told me that if we sell them out of the state to small time gun stores, it's highly unlikely they would make their way back here into the hands of future competitors plus, you make a little money."

The crowd once again began talking amongst themselves as Judge Reeves banged the gavel asking for silence, "Continue, Mr. Palumbo."

Rico continued, "So he sent me to do that and I was out of the city for a few weeks and it was my job to watch out for any new street gun sellers."

Mr. Levine turned to the jury, "So we have someone illegally selling firearms, who is aware that possibly murder was involved and never turned them over to the police. Instead he conveniently shipped them out of state, took a quick bit of cash, and ran off with it. Mr. Harry Goodrich may be rich but I think that the various witnesses should make it clear that he isn't good. This is a clear and obvious pattern take over, manipulate, make money and who cares how many people die as a result of these firearms being sold under the table across the country."

Mr. Levine stepped down as Ms. James stood up, rolling her eyes, "Does anyone actually believe this person? Our district attorney is using someone who should be in jail for accessory to murder and obstruction of justice to get someone who committed a far lesser crime. The crime they claim my client was involved with was selling weapons to people who would themselves most likely sell them legally to people after a background check. This man knowingly loaned them to people knowing they would kill people in at least some cases and sent them to someone to destroy the evidence. They wonder why Covenant City had one of the highest murder rates per capita in the country."

She walked closer to the jury and began pacing back and forth in front of them. "Ladies and gentlemen of the jury, our justice system isn't perfect, sometimes we have to do plea bargains, but when we do they might spare a thief to capture a murderer. This however is backwards, the person who sold the guns directly to potential murderers is being given a pass to capture my client who stopped it? Does that make sense to anyone in this room? Quite frankly it doesn't – what I think this should show is that this trial is not about justice or about cleaning up the street, this is something else. This is something that is driven by selfishness and personal interest. The public good be damned. I think we should all wonder what would make our district attorney who is supposed to be working for the people of Covenant City and this low life join forces against this man who supposedly committed a lesser crime? I don't know but if you judge someone by who they associate with our district attorney has a lot to answer for."

The crowd in the room began to talk about what they had just heard and once again Judge Reeves had to ask for silence. Judge Reeves then said, "Do you have any questions for the witness?"

Ms. James turned to Rico and said, "Yes, I have a few questions. One, how long did you do this before my client supposedly shut you down? Two, how many guns did you rent? Third, say you rent 10 guns, how many of them do you believe were used for murder? I think this court would be very curious to know how much blood is on your hands."

Mr. Levine immediately leapt to his feet, "Objection! This trial is about Mr. Harry Goodrich, not this witness, this line of questioning is a pointless distraction."

Judge Reeves paused, "Ms. James, I believe you have already made your point and while it is certainly worth looking into that is not the point of this trial today."

Ms. James annoyed, turned and said, "Very well then, in that case no more questions your Honour."

Ms. James sat down next to Harry and made a quick note before Judge Reeves called for a brief recess before the next round of testimony. Ms. James whispered to Harry, "I'm glad you agreed to the jury because I have a bad feeling about Judge Reeves, she's being subtle but something's not right."

Harry Goodrich whispered back, "You're getting that vibe too? I was wondering if I was being paranoid."

She whispered back, "If the judge can shut down our dialogue and is intentionally doing so, this is going to be a lot harder."

Harry whispered to her, "Don't worry too much, I chose the best attorney I know to represent me. Even if the judge is trying to tip the scale, we can use that to our advantage."

Witness: Katie Guerrero

They returned from the recess and the next person called to the witness stand was Katie Guerrero, a long-time friend of Harry Goodrich. She was sworn in and Ms. James approached the witness stand, "Katie, how long have you known Mr. Goodrich?"

She responded, "I have known him for 20 years and I can't believe that we are even talking about the same person that the last two witnesses described."

Ms. James, "So you have known him before he supposedly took over this gang and supposedly became the crime lord that the prosecution alleges."

Katie responded, "Yes, I met Harry in high school and he was always there to help people, he was always there to do things to help people. I remember one time when we were in grade 12, these three grade 11 kids were shoving a ninth grader into a locker and he stood up to them. They got in his face telling him to mind his own business, and he told them if they leave that kid alone he would. Just when it seemed like a fight was going to break out they said to him 'Why are you starting a fight you can't win?' He said to them, 'I was about to ask you the same thing, because you can't win, if you kick my ass, everyone will know you are cowards who ganged up on one guy, if I kick all yours you are wusses, so why are you starting a fight you can't win?' They had no answer, they were totally lost, they backed off and walked away, he helped the kid out of his locker and even walked him home that day. That is the man I know, someone who is willing to risk his safety for the well-being of others."

Ms. James stood there, "Well that is a lovely story but admittedly that was over 20 years ago, do you have any examples that are more recent?"

She said, "Of course, he actually sponsors charity runs and dozens of people. I bet he's raised thousands of dollars over the last few years for various charities. He has even donated to the local police in the past, what crime boss would fund the people he is fighting? He once told me a story about how he looked at a search engine of charities in the country and he was overwhelmed."

Ms. James probed, "What do you mean overwhelmed?"

Katie answered, "He was both glad to see so many people trying to make things better but also heartbroken because the problems of the world are so big that even with all those people working on it the problems still weren't solved."

Ms. James looked back at the jury to see whether they were being won over, the looks on their faces ranged from unconvinced to feeling conflicted about what they were hearing. She decided to keep going, "So have you ever seen him act in a way that is manipulative or exploitative of people?"

Katie responded, "Absolutely not, he is very intelligent and ambitious but he is always trying to do the right thing, he once said to me that the richest man in the world will never be the happiest until he does good with his wealth."

Ms. James continued, "So what would you tell the jury about the charges and the stories you have heard today?"

She responded, "It's just plain stupid."

Ms. James placed a hand on the judge's stand leaning in to say, "No further questions Your Honour."

Ms. James walked away as Mr. Levine stood up and approached the witness stand, "I want to ask you a question, is he really the sweet, caring, just person that you say he is?"

Katie responded, "Of course."

Mr. Levine said, "Okay, if you have been his friend all of these years then I want you to tell us all his most embarrassing personal story."

Ms. James stood up, "Objection, this has no relevance to this case!"

Judge Reeves got a concerned look on her face, "Mr. Levine, please explain what this has to do with this case?"

Mr. Levine responded, "Very simple Your Honour, if he is the crime boss that I say he is, he would never let an embarrassing story come out in such a public forum because crime bosses function off of fear and intimidation."

Ms. James stood up again, "Your Honour this is pathetic, no one wants embarrassing stories told about them in public. This is the saddest excuse of questioning I have heard in my years as a criminal defense attorney."

Judge Reeves looked back at Mr. Levine, "I'm afraid I have to agree, if you have no other questions, then we should move on."

He grimaced with frustration as he said, "Okay, one of the things you said interested me. On the first day of this trial we saw footage of him trying to get a job for Mr. Ethan Sawyer. Why would he offer that man a job and not other people? Isn't it possible that he owed him something, a favour."

Katie continued, "Like I said, he always want to help people. The only thing that last witness said that was true was that he was full of interesting phrases. He used to say, 'I wish I knew how to never have another recession.' I asked him why and he said 'It scares me to think of how many people get knocked down every time it happens and never get back up.' That is the person I know and am proud to consider my friend."

Mr. Levine turned away from her with a long pause, "Mrs. Guerrero, isn't it just too convenient that all of these people have come forward and more to come now that we have him in custody. Shouldn't that strike you as odd for an innocent man?"

Katie responded, "You've assembled quite the collection, but I'd have to see it to believe it, lots of people claim to be abducted by aliens, seen Bigfoot, there are conventions for people who think the earth is flat. Until you provide hard evidence, all you have is a myth."

Shocked by her response, Mr. Levine peered at the jury who seemed impressed by the answer. Mr. Levine turned to the judge, "No further questions Your Honour."

Mr. Levine went back to his seat, as Katie got up from the witness stand and shook Harry's hand before leaving the courtroom.

Harry looked confidently at Ms. James, nodding in approval.

Witness: Rod Wendall

A tough looking muscular man approached the witness stand, his hair stood straight up and his beard around his mouth and on his chin was dark and thick. He was sworn in and Mr. Levine approached the witness stand. "Mr. Wendall, would you mind telling the court what you did?"

Rod responded, "Well before the Halloween from Hell I was hired muscle, if you needed to break someone's hand for not paying their debts, I did it. If you needed someone to have your back because you were dealing with someone you didn't trust too much, I did that too. When the Halloween from Hell happened I was shot twice and I spent hours in surgery getting those bullets taken out of me and my intestines getting sewn up. After about a month I get a call saying that the new boss wanted to speak to me, so I'm expecting the same old, same old."

He was suddenly interrupted by Mr. Levine, "So who was the new boss?"

Rod pointed right at Harry Goodrich, "That's him right there."

The audience began to talk as Judge Reeves banged her gavel. "Silence, it's been a long day, please, Mr. Levine continue."

Mr. Levine nodded, "Thank you, Your Honour."

He then put his hand on the rail of the witness stand, "So the new boss, Mr. Goodrich, calls you into his office and what does he offer you?"

Rod continued, "He starts telling me about how the old system didn't work but that he was putting together a new one, he also said that he wanted me to take on a new role. I asked him what it was, he said, 'How would you like to be a bodyguard for women, against wife beaters, rapists, and stalkers.' I ask him what it pays, he asks me what my rate is, I tell him, he says that he will offer me a little less per job but he can get me enough volume to make up for it. I ask him, 'What if I refuse?' He responds, 'You'll have to leave town because we're the only game in town and the job you used to do is going to be obsolete.' So I thought about it and I asked him, 'How are you going to find these women?' He says, 'Don't worry about it, your job is to be the supply, let me worry about finding the demand.' I started to look at other towns because I thought this wouldn't last, but it did. He found the clients, I don't know why he chose those clients but he did."

Mr. Levine asked, "So tell me, how did you know who you were guarding?"

Rod responded, "I only met Harry two or three times and he was always texting me the details."

Mr. Levine went to the evidence, "Your Honour, on that phone are a couple dozen texts clearly explaining his most recent assignments and general banter about how each job went."

The judge looked through the phone, nodding as she read through the various texts. After Judge Reeves handed the phone back to Mr. Levine who placed it back on the evidence table. "Mr. Levine please continue."

Mr. Levine followed up, "So, you became the bodyguard, tell me, did you ever assault anyone during this time?"

Rod answered, "Yes, one guy, the woman I was assigned to was a couple of days away from moving across the country so that this guy wouldn't find her. The last time she had seen him, he told her that she was coming with him either in the front seat or the trunk. She was convinced this guy was going to kill her, which is why she agreed to our service. I'm walking her from her job to the day care where her son was. We get to the daycare and the ex-boyfriend was there yelling at the person behind the desk, that he was taking his kid and that is all there was to it.

"He turns around and sees her, I was walking in the door when he swung at her, she got out of the way and I knocked that guy down. He got back up and asked who I was, I told him 'I'm the guy keeping her safe from you.' He gets up and tries to attack me again this time I knocked him out he went down and he was unconscious. Thanks to that, she had all the evidence she needed to get her kid and we then recommended a safe house where we had a few other people who were hiding out, and by the time he got out of the hospital she was already on her way across the country and he was out of luck."

Mr. Levine followed up, "So, what you are saying basically is that Mr. Goodrich took a hired gun, and instead of you threatening or beating up people who are in debt you were beating up stalkers for desperate women who were in extremely dangerous circumstances?"

Rod responded, "Yeah, that's pretty much it. It was easier than the drug deals because the other guy usually wasn't packing."

Mr. Levine quickly followed up, "You mean they usually weren't armed?"

Rod responded, "Yes."

Mr. Levine turned to the jury, "Ladies and gentlemen, isn't this interesting, under the guise of benevolence this man was taking advantage of families in the most desperate and tragic of circumstances. Make no mistake, this isn't about doing better for the community, this isn't about anything other than business. That's all, cold hard business and playing with the lives of innocent people. In closing, this is wrong, we need to stop this, Covenant City deserves better."

Mr. Levine stepped away and sat down at his table as Judge Reeves told Ms. James to approach the witness stand.

Ms. James approached the stand, "Ladies and gentlemen, while Mr. Levine was trying to pull on your heartstrings his story has more than a few loose ends."

A small laugh went across the courtroom. "Mr. Wendall, first of all, isn't it odd that for someone who is trying to re-brand this supposed crime syndicate, he would hire you, who quite frankly looks like a stereotypical thug."

Mr. Levine stood up, "Objection, the witness's looks are irrelevant."

Ms. James turned to Judge Reeves, "Actually in this case they are, if you are trying to change over a store, you would make sure that you change the layout. You would hire different employees or at the very least make them wear a different uniform."

Ms. James turned to the jury, "However, that is just the beginning, ladies and gentlemen of the jury. Even according to their stories many of these women were desperate and fleeing for their lives, what money did they have to pay? This witness has no clue, even though he did this for years. I've heard of staying inside the job description but this is ignorance of the highest order." A few more laughs came out. "Perhaps what is the most puzzling thing is that I have not heard any evidence outside of your testimony that you even knew this man, much less worked for him. What evidence do you have?"

Rod responded, "I already gave you my phone so you can see it for yourself."

Ms. James went over to the witness stand, "This phone, the one with the text messages from a few people most notably the ones named 'Harry Goodrich,' for a long time thug like yourself, that seems too obvious doesn't it? Besides, Harry would you please take out your cell phone and turn it on?"

Harry took out his cell phone and placed it on the table, where Ms. James picked it up. She asked for a volunteer from the jury who had raised his hand, she placed it in his hand and said, "Please tell me when it is on and the ringer is at maximum volume."

The juror agreed and did so, "Okay."

She gave Boris' phone to another juror, instructing, "Call the number assigned to Mr. Goodrich, if it rings you have your answer, if not well then I guess we'll be bothering someone else."

The juror pressed the call button next to Harry Goodrich's name, with microphones next to each phone and waited, one ring after another went by with Harry's phone remaining silent. She put down Harry's phone as she waited for the voice-mail message to come up and a woman's voice came onto the phone. "Hi this is Maxine, I'm sorry I missed your call, just leave your name and number after the beep and I'll get back to you as soon as possible, thanks."

There was a loud beep as the juror ended the call and Ms. James turned to Rod, "Would you mind telling us who Maxine is?"

Rod was very confused, "I don't know maybe it's his secretary or something."

Ms. James responded, "Your Honour, Mr. Goodrich's secretary is named Alicia and does not sound like that. In any event, this is not Mr. Goodrich's cell phone, I will happily provide four year's worth of phone bills to prove that his number is not that one, and the number on Mr. Wendall's cell phone is going to someone else, it could be his girlfriend for all we know."

Judge Reeve's turned back to Rod, "Is there anything you forgot to tell me or anyone else in this court today?"

Rod was stunned, looking to Mr. Levine for guidance when Judge Reeves said in a louder tone, "Hey look at me. Is there anything you forgot to tell us today in this court?"

Rod was speechless, Mr. Levine's face was in his hands as he was overwhelmed with embarrassment at having his client's story torn apart. Judge Reeves said, "Mr. Wendall please leave the witness stand."

He got up and walked out feeling completely embarrassed as Judge Reeves addressed everyone in the court, "I would like to make something very clear, there are a lot of wild stories flying around this courtroom and quite frankly I have had my fill of them for today. Furthermore, Mr. Levine please do a better job verifying your evidence. While I can't speak for the jury, from my perspective, up to this point all you have provided is questionable and inconsistent testimony. We will resume trial a week from this upcoming Thursday."

She banged her gavel as the crowd began to talk to each other about what had just occurred.

Just as Mr. Levine picked up his briefcase, his hands with their white knuckles showing his frustration, as he marched out in fury.

Ms. James whispered to Harry, "Please tell me you are seeing what I am, he's on wobbly legs and is one big shot from going down for the count."

Harry was unable to share her joy there was a dead silence from him, she turned to him, "What's going on?"

He moved his head towards the door, indicating his desire to speak elsewhere.

Between the Second and Third Day of the Trial

Between the Second and Third Day of the Trial

Just as the limousine door closed, Harry began by saying, "First of all, great touch engaging the jury, brilliant move."

Ms. James responded, "Thanks, I am still not sure that Judge Reeves isn't trying to lightly tip the scale. What was it you wanted to talk about?"

He responded, "We won the battle but we might lose the war. I better take a few precautions just in case."

Ms. James asked, "What type of precautions?"

He responded as he picked up a glass of champagne. "I don't know, I'm still deciding."

It was the Friday morning, six days before the third day of the trial Harry Goodrich was closing the safe behind the painting in his office, when Alicia spoke into his intercom. "Harry, Kevin is here to see you."

Harry responded, "Just a moment."

The door opened as he was moving the painting back to his original position. Kevin walked in, Harry looked at him confused, "Didn't I say just a minute?"

Kevin trying to act on his feet, "I didn't hear that part."

Harry responded, "Okay, I called you here because I got some really strange news, I think somebody in our organization is feeding information to our beloved district attorney."

The sarcasm that emerged was only overpowered by his disgust, after a brief moment Harry continued, "I don't know who it is yet, but here is the deal, if something happens to me I want to give you this."

He held up a big key painted a metallic blue, "Just in case Levine has more information than he has let on and I end up going to jail, use that key. It will open up the safe that's behind me. It'll have everything you need, but if I don't go to jail then just give it back to me and everything will be back to business as usual."

Kevin said, "Thank you sir, this is a tremendous Honour."

Harry responded, "Well when everything is at stake you have to pick your friends carefully and sometimes you just have to trust people and I

The Great Gangster

have confidence in you. Don't tell anyone about that key or that I have chosen you to be my successor, I don't want there to be a target on you if I go to jail and the wrong people find out you have the key."

Harry let out a loud breath, "It would be bad, you understand right?"

Kevin said, "Yes, absolutely, thank you so much. You can count on me, this key is in safe hands."

Kevin picked up the key and left, just as he was walking out the door Harry turned to the receptionist Alicia and said to her, "Just in case things turn out badly, take your three weeks of vacation and make sure you start it no later than the last day of the trial."

She said to him, "Everything is going to be okay right?"

He responded, "You know me, hope for the best but prepare for the worst."

With two days until the trial, Harry went over to Ms. James house, she welcomed him in. She began, "Unfortunately the fear of a return to the way things used to be is to his advantage but I think we have shown enough reasonable doubt until this point."

Harry responded, "Who is he bringing up this time?"

Ms. James responded, "I don't know, they are keeping that person's identity a secret, whoever it is, we have to frame it as a desperate cowardly act. Beyond that, we have to rip apart any story the witness is telling."

Harry responded, "What if this person has the evidence that we can't argue against? All the TV shows make it look like a performance and you are a tremendous performer, but what if they have too much?"

Ms. James responded, "We have Dr. Martin, by the time she finishes telling her story you will be a saint to those jurors."

Harry then said, "I know it's not conventional, but if we need it, should you call me to the witness stand?"

Ms. James said, "No, absolutely not, that is exactly what Levine wants. He would salivate over that opportunity, I am telling you we don't need that."

Harry responded, "I hope you're right, either way that is going to be one hard day."

The Third and Final Day of the Trial

Witness: Dr. Judy Martin

Ms. James called up her final witness to the stand, Dr. Judy Martin, who was a gynecologist from Virginia and was there to testify on Harry's behalf. Ms. James asked Dr. Martin to begin telling her story.

"When you work in an abortion clinic, you get a lot of protests, threats and other things. One day, I was driving home and I noticed that someone had been following me since I left the building. I had to call the police to say someone was following me. Eventually I pulled into the police station and I thought I would be safe there, instead this lunatic comes in and starts yelling at me, calling me a murderer and that I should be killed. I pressed charges against that person but it still scared me and I seriously contemplated shutting down my practice. How many more people are like that? What if they find out where I live?"

The jurors looked on with sympathy and shock as she spoke of her troubling experiences. "We always had people protesting, and some of our staff would quit after being mailed threatening letters, it made things really hard and the police didn't come to help very often. It was around the time of the lunatic following me home that we considered shutting down the clinic for our safety. Around that time we had a phone call from someone working with a lot of women, and this person asked if we would be willing to send someone to look after the women."

"And this person who called you, turned out to be Harry Goodrich?" Ms. James asked.

"Yes. I told him that we were struggling to keep our staffing where it was, he then responded 'Why is that?' I told him about the threats we get and there was a long pause and he said that he would send us some security. I asked if they could handle the pressure, protests and threats, he responded, 'They are former soldiers, some of the people who protest will feel guilty for giving them a hard time and they won't be intimidated.' I wasn't sure but I knew how badly the women who come here need our services, and the next nearest clinic is over an hour away, and some of our patients don't have a car. Without us they struggle, so when you are in that situation you are thankful for any help you can get."

Ms. James smirked, "So, how long did you and your colleagues participate in this agreement?"

Judy continued, "For the last four years, and I am so glad we did, things started to change immediately; the protestors began to go away and the threats began to fall off. The worst incident was a few months after, when one guy came up and tried to attack one of our patients and the security tackled the guy immediately and he was taken away. If it hadn't been for that I don't know what we would have done, our turnover slowed and we began to be able to provide more services for our patients and others."

Ms. James confidently turned to the jury, "So, you provided your services to some of the employees of Mr. Goodrich, did you see anything that was illegal or troubling?"

Judy continued, "No, the women were happy, healthy, and they never hesitated to ask me any questions or concerns they may have had. As far as I can tell, Mr. Goodrich is an employer who cares about women's issues and put his money where his mouth is to back up those beliefs."

Ms. James said to Judge Reeves, "No further questions your Honour," as she sat down.

Judge Reeves turned to Mr. Levine, "Do you have any questions for Dr. Martin?"

Mr. Levine stood up and approached the bench, "As a matter of fact I do. We already know Mr. Goodrich isn't above getting people to do his dirty work Dr. Martin, how do you know he wasn't behind the stalker incident you described?"

Judy responded, "Even if he was behind it, the harassment that I, my colleagues and our patients receive from many people on a regular basis is absolutely sickening. No matter how desperate their situation is, no matter how difficult it may be, we are ripped to shreds by supposedly pro-life people who want to see us shut down so more babies are born, but stop giving a damn if the child dies at age 3 for any reason. The fact is, I go to my job every day knowing that I can safely perform my job, and our security not only helped us be safer but they actually helped us come up with ways to be even more secure."

Mr. Levine rolled his eyes, "That is very nice, but don't you think it is a little suspicious that he called just after such a serious incident? Isn't it too much of a coincidence?"

Judy responded, "He could have called at any time, that's the point, it is constant. I hope you never go home at night driving twenty minutes out of your way so you drive by a police station so that if someone seems to be following you, you can get out of there before something happens. That was our lives, he and his colleagues helped us live safer lives, what are you doing besides wasting everyone's time?"

The onlookers let out a mild chuckle as Mr. Levine's patience began to dissipate, "Okay Dr. Martin, and before I ask this, I need to remind you that you are under oath, meaning if you intentionally lie you will be charged with perjury."

Dr. Martin's eyes lit up with anger, "I know all about oaths and I don't appreciate you talking down to me."

Judge Reeves intervened with the tension rising, "Mr. Levine, please stay on topic and ask your questions."

Mr. Levine nodded, "Dr. Martin, why did he reach out to your firm, than say gynecologists, or other women's health professionals here in Vermont? Is it possible he was taking advantage of your desperate situation so that you could provide some pretend health care to the women trapped in his prostitution ring?"

Judy rolled her eyes, "First of all, I didn't ask what they did for work, it was none of my business. He told my colleague, who handled most of the communication and the large majority of the visits, that he just wanted to help us and his employees in a win-win situation. Also, those women weren't trapped anywhere, besides if this was some pimp, he wouldn't bother getting them health care – and not from professionals. These women were sexually active, but guess what, it's part of life... for most of us anyway."

The crowd let out another chuckle, Mr. Levine was very unsatisfied, "So you took a job, not asking why, or should I say settling for a stupid answer, and now you are just going to play ignorant? You are a medical professional, you can't expect me or this court to believe that you didn't see what was going on down there. I am going to ask you one more time, were you providing medical services to Mr. Goodrich's prostitution ring?"

Dr. Martin stared at him, "I don't know what their occupation was, nor is it my business, even if I did it is covered by doctor patient confidentiality. I took an oath to do no harm and not to run people's lives for them. I have already said what I know, what happened, and how I know Mr. Goodrich, which isn't very well. He never threatened me, we had a couple of short but pleasant conversations, and that is it. If I tell you anything past that then I would be making things up so now you would be asking me to commit perjury, which is that thing where you lie under oath."

Mr. Levine spoke up, "Objection, hostile witness."

Judge Reeves banged her gavel, "Dr. Martin, you may step down, and Mr. Levine I hope your future lines of questioning are not so antagonizing in nature."

He went back to his seat while Ms. James whispered in Harry's ear, "He is on the ropes. Unless he has a trump card, we can knock him out on the final statements and go home happy."

Final Witness

Judge Reeves declared to the courtroom, "I think we have heard a lot from this case over the last couple of weeks, so unless either side has anymore witnesses or evidence to present to the court, then we can move on to the final statements and the jury's decision."

Ms. James stood up, "I have no further witnesses or questions, unless Mr. Levine has anything he wishes to bring up."

Judge Reeves nodded turning to Mr. Levine, who looked over at Harry Goodrich and winked, before turning back Judge Reeves and walking towards the room near the back of the courtroom. Mr. Levine proudly declared, "Please bring in my final witness."

Kevin Alvarez emerged from the back room while Harry looked at him with great disappointment. Kevin sat on the witness stand and was sworn in, with each passing second, Harry became more and more disgusted and Ms. James became concerned.

Mr. Levine started, "Would you please state your name for the court and how you know Mr. Goodrich?"

Kevin went on, "Well my name is Kevin Alvarez and I worked for Mr. Goodrich in both his legal and illegal operations for the last four years. Pretty much since the January after the Halloween from Hell."

Mr. Levine went on, "So, would you please tell the court what capacity you served in?"

Kevin continued, "I helped manage his operations, he was running multiple schemes in a city with almost a million people. I dealt with him multiple times a week and I was one of his closest allies in so many of his schemes."

Mr. Levine continued on, "Would you mind telling us how he ran all these schemes?"

Kevin responded, "Certainly, he came back after the Halloween from Hell and completely reorganized the whole game and started us off on an entirely different path. All of the stuff about the guns being sent out of state, the prostitution, the way that he gave cheap rehab, all of it is true. I had never seen this before and I used to ask him, 'Why are we doing things this way? If we play our cards right we can hold onto these customers while pulling in new ones and we could make a fortune.' If he said it once he must have said it a dozen times, 'No, if the illegal markets get too big it invites competition, and competition is unacceptable in our industry. The reason why competition works in the other industries is because they play by rules, we don't.' This part he loved to bring up in particular, 'Could you imagine if Coke and Pepsi didn't play by rules and were willing to kill for every street corner?' He thought that we needed to keep it small and help people up and out of their desperate circumstances because he was convinced that a new wave of them was always just around the corner."

Mr. Levine asked, "So his business model for lack of a better term was designed to capitalize on our city's desperate people and trying to monopolize organized crime in the city?"

Kevin nodded, "Exactly, I will say this, he was careful and he was clever."

Mr. Levine gave a sarcastic puzzled face, "What are you referring to exactly?"

Kevin responded, "He was so careful, he made sure all of us had laptop computers and trained us how to destroy the hard drive beyond repair in less than five seconds. He made sure that we never sent e-mails or letters, that would minimize any paper trail. Boris and Rod were the exceptions, they were always on his list of people he could cut on a moment's notice. He didn't trust them, which was why he had the alternate text system and the letters, while having information, never had any information on it that could be traced to him."

Mr. Levine looked over and saw the jurors hanging on to Kevin's every word.

"Most of all, all of the laptops had their internet drive disabled so that we couldn't send e-mails or get our documents caught by anybody. He did a lot of his business with these," Kevin held up several USB drives and asked that each one be inserted into a computer that Mr. Levine brought that was plugged into a projector screen.

The entire courtroom was captivated as Mr. Levine had a smug grin on his face and began setting up the presentation. "Mr. Alvarez would you please explain to the court what we are looking at?"

Kevin Alvarez began, "First here, is the list of agents and their performance in terms of selling marijuana. He didn't just want to know how much you were selling and how much money, he always wanted you to talk the person up."

Mr. Levine asked, "Well why is that?"

Kevin continued, "Because depending on your circumstances, we could send you towards our other programs. This chart here shows

The Great Gangster

who we gave cheap rehab to. This one here is who we offered low level jobs to and this one who we gave financial counselling to. Some people make enough but don't manage it well."

Mr. Levine probed further, "So he continued to sell marijuana to people to find vulnerable people to fund his other operations and find others who he could up-sell his other operations to?"

Kevin continued, "Exactly, one business would feed into another, the security for the clinics down in Virginia were homeless ex-soldiers. In exchange for their service he gave them some money and his unofficial forms of treatment."

Mr. Levine continued, "Such as?"

Kevin was ready to burst with the next sentence, "We had leftover magic mushrooms and other hallucinogens. We gave it to these soldiers while keeping them under observation because it would supposedly help them with their PTSD. He got some college students who were studying this stuff in school to give them cheap counselling in exchange for the references and some money to pay down their student loans with."

Mr. Levine, "Wow, what were some of the other ways he interconnected the businesses?"

Kevin continued, "Well those gynecologists he gave protection to would check on the prostitutes and the strippers to keep them happy and healthy, and he did give them a college fund out of the money they raised. He always said, 'Whether we like it or not, a lot of people looking for prostitutes are looking for young. If we don't create a constructive exit plan responsible, healthy women will not want to work for us and we will only be getting the desperate ones, which may one day dry up if they ever fix some of these economic issues.' He also used to say, 'If another pimp comes to town, we should be the women's first choice so that those old style pimps don't have a chance.' He actually was so insistent on destroying competition, he had a first report policy, where if one of the older women who did reception heard any of the clients claiming our prices were higher than someone, we would report to him what we could find out."

Mr. Levine, with great enthusiasm, asked, "Then what would happen?"

Kevin continued, "Very simple, he finds out who it is, he sends a woman willing to risk herself to make a big bonus. Then she tells that pimp that she wants to start working with him, she scopes the place out for a week, two weeks, no more than a month. Then one day the cops show up, mass arrests happen, and she conveniently tells the guy the night before that her sister died and she has to go to the funeral.

The Great Gangster

The pimp goes to jail, the women who were working for him are either jailed or freed depending on how they got there, and now the johns who didn't get busted go right back to us. Sometimes the prostitutes who did get busted would come back to us and use our loans for legal services."

Mr. Levine then asked, "What I don't understand is why didn't your operations get caught until recently?"

Just before responding, Kevin looked over at Harry Goodrich who was shaking his head with great disappointment. "He didn't start this from scratch, both the Italians and the Russians already had cops in their pockets. As the only game in town, he kept some of the extra cash flowing their way and every now and then the cops would try to bust a place and they would get there too late."

Kevin started laughing, "One time just to mess with your office, one of our guys gave a tip that they were running money laundering, and people were walking out with thousands of dollars of laundered money every night between seven and eight pm at 4136 Sycamore Avenue, the retirement home where your parents were. In reality the only big money being delivered was on Wheel of Fortune." Kevin continued laughing, "I would have paid $20 to see the expression on your face when you read that."

Mr. Levine turned around and gave a smiling scowl at Harry Goodrich, before turning to the jury and continuing, "So now that these operations have been exposed, the few fake stores that they launder the money through can be seen for what they are – a cancer on our city. They took advantage of those who were most desperate and mocked and corrupted our law enforcement in the process. I hope you now can all see Mr. Goodrich is rich but he isn't so good after all. No further questions Your Honour."

Judge Reeves turned to the defence, "Ms. James do you have any questions for the witness?"

Ms. James walked up the bench, "Yes I do, Your Honour, I have to ask two big questions to Mr. Alvarez, why did you keep your witness status a secret until this very moment?"

Mr. Levine stood up, "Your Honour, that was my idea. Due to the danger of testifying against crime bosses, you have to keep these people secret so that my client wouldn't be threatened, assaulted, or killed before his testimony."

Ms. James turned back to Kevin Alvarez, "Well Kevin, my other question is, why now, why after all these years would you testify against Mr. Goodrich? Why now would you suddenly decide to speak out against the crime in our city?"

He disingenuously responded, "Because I care about our city and I just couldn't stand to see it in the hands of that man any longer."

He had pointed at Harry Goodrich, and Ms. James turned to Judge Reeves, "Your Honour, this isn't legitimate testimony, Mr. Alvarez is doing a favour for Mr. Levine's office and I can only imagine what he was offered for it."

Mr. Levine stood up yelling, "I object! My office is trying to prosecute a top level criminal and we are doing what we have to do to clean up our streets."

Ms. James turned suddenly to Mr. Levine, "How many rats are you letting run free because you hate this raccoon so much?"

Judge Reeves took over, banging her gavel, "I would like to remind both of you this is a court proceeding and personal attacks between attorneys do not belong here and is not becoming of your position Ms. James. Mr. Alvarez you may step down."

Ms. James objected, "Your Honour, I am not finished my questions."

Judge Reeves responded, "This line of questioning has devolved into personal attacks. Nothing else can come from this and we will take a brief recess before the prosecution and defence make their respective closing statements."

Ms. James walked back to the defence table visibly upset as she said to Harry, "Sorry, I should have been more careful. I gave Judge Reeves an opening to shut down our questioning, damn."

Harry responded, "I was afraid of this."

Ms. James responded, "You were afraid Kevin Alvarez was the witness?"

Harry responded, "No, I was afraid of what would happen if they had the evidence, and what would happen to the city without me."

Kevin Alvarez
Outside of Court

Kevin was rushed and escorted out of court to a nearby vehicle, as soon as he got in the vehicle he said to the driver, "Take me to Mr. Goodrich's office, 763 Presley Street."

He texted his girlfriend, "The testimony went great, Harry didn't see it coming, he never thought I would work with Levine and now the business is all mine."

She responded, "I can't wait for all the limos and money you are going to get, you have wanted this for a long time."

He responded with three texts, "Ever since the Halloween from Hell, the problem was he moved first, I waited too long to begin building my group and so if I didn't join him I was out-gunned."

His second text added, "At first I thought I could enjoy being a second in command but he was always playing too nice and dismissing me."

His third text read, "Now I'm the boss and I'm one stop from getting the last thing I need."

Just as they were pulling onto Presley Street he got a phone call from Mr. Levine, "Great job Kevin, he's got nothing to defend with now."

Kevin responded, "Is that full immunity document ready?"

Mr. Levine responded, "Tomorrow morning, it will be printed, signed and notarized, but remember we may need more testimony if he gets an appeal."

Kevin responded, "No problem, pleasure doing business with you. This November you have my vote."

Kevin hung up, chuckling to himself as he got out of the car. When he got to the office door, he saw a different woman at the reception desk, and he asked her, "I'm sorry, who are you? I've never seen you before."

The meek woman responded, "I'm Maxine. Alicia took an extended vacation for three weeks, she told me not to let anyone into Mr. Goodrich's office unless he is here."

The Great Gangster

Kevin responded, "Well, I'm the boss now, everything I need to run the show is in the safe in his office and I have the key to open it with."

She stood up while she asked him to stop but he opened the side of his jacket revealing the gun he had there, "Now you just stay right there and do your job and everything will be just fine."

Seriously intimidated, she sat down, as he opened the door and closed it behind him, looking around the room proud of his conquest. He sat down on Harry's chair and put his hands behind his head while putting his feet on the desk. He looked at the door, thinking to himself, "Everyone coming through that door is going to be doing what I say from now on."

He then stood up, moved the painting behind him out of the way and that was where he saw the safe that had the keyhole. He pulled out the metallic blue key, bracing himself for the power that hid inside that safe. He inserted the key and turned it, he opened the safe only to see a slightly smaller one, with a folded note in front of it. On the outside of the note it said, "16, 33, 10, 31, 5, read the note while waiting for the time release lock to open." He turned the knob to the different numbers finally hearing the ticking noise while he opened the note to read what was inside:

"Kevin Alvarez, if you are reading this you have betrayed me, I suspected it because I knew that these witnesses were coming from within the organization. People who always whined and complained about my way of doing things, just like you. You were always so nostalgic for the old days of Covenant City, you were always trying to push me back in that direction believing it would make us bigger and richer than ever. I guess you forgot what else it brings…"

Kevin began to wonder what he was talking about when a loud noise came from inside the safe, the door swung open with a handgun falling forward aiming right at Kevin, causing him to scream, immediately duck down, and cover his head.

He was shaking and so shocked it took him a few seconds to realize there had been no gun shot, or noise of any kind. He slowly pulled himself up beside where the gun was to see inside the smaller safe. He finally looked inside to see the small light bulb inside illuminating the black letters at the back of the small safe: "The opening of this safe has sent a signal and now Kevin Alvarez, you have a hit on you. You won't know whether it is a man, woman, child, machine, or animal, you are now a marked man. You wanted the old days back, well, you should have been more careful what you wished for!"

Kevin immediately panicked, rushing out the door to see Maxine driving away. He immediately looked around realizing that he might be

The Great Gangster

alone in the building with the assassin. He immediately charged out of the building. He got into the car that was still waiting outside and told his driver, "Take me home, now."

He looked around frantically suddenly realizing that if someone as careful and intricate Harry Goodrich was putting a hit on someone it literally could come from anyone, anywhere, anytime. He suddenly changed his mind, "On second thought, new plan, turn around and go to Levine's office."

As they drove, he nervously watched for any sign of a car following them or a vehicle that might run into them. He even asked his driver what the exact route was in case the driver had other plans. Finally, he pulled up to Mr. Levine's office frantically asking to see him as someone told him to take a seat in his office and settle down.

As his jacket swayed the assistant could see his gun and whispered, "Mr. Alvarez, you cannot bring a gun into Mr. Levine's office. Please leave it in your car."

He nervously nodded his head, ran back to his car and put his gun in the back seat and told the driver, "Don't let anyone touch this gun, I don't know who we can trust."

Kevin walked back in as the assistant led him into the room where he sat down on the chair facing Mr. Levine's desk and began to catch his breath.

Kevin asked, "Who are you?"

The assistant quickly responded, "Jay," and asked, "Why are you so scared? What happened?"

Kevin, looking over his shoulder said, "Harry Goodrich put a hit out on me, I don't know if it is a man, a woman, a child, a machine, an animal – it could be anything. That's why I'm here, I need Levine to arrange to get me into the witness protection program or something. When will he be back?"

Jay responded, "Well we have to wait for the jury to come to their decision which shouldn't take too long… you traitor."

Final Statements

Judge Reeves came out to say, "Before the jurors go to reach their verdict, do we have any final statements from counsel?"

Mr. Levine rose, "Ladies and gentlemen of the jury, my hope is that you are now fully aware of Mr. Goodrich's crimes against this community and the evidence provided by Mr. Alvarez paints that picture very clearly. I hope that all of you remember what is at stake, this isn't just one bad apple, our city has made tremendous progress while people like him are a cancer that must be removed before their influence and corruption spread. It should be clear that Mr. Goodrich is guilty of every single charge in question. The fate of Covenant City is in your hands and given the case that has been made I have the utmost confidence that you will make the right decision."

Judge Reeves asked, "Would the defence like to make a closing statement?"

As Ms. James stood up, Harry put his arm on her shoulder, "I want to say this myself."

Ms. James looked confused, "are you sure?"

Harry nodded, "Very sure."

Ms. James addressed the court, "Your Honour, my client would like to make this statement himself."

Judge Reeves nodded, saying, "Proceed."

Harry stood up and walked to the centre of the courtroom to face the jury straight in front of him. He glanced over his shoulder at Mr. Levine as if to say, "Watch this."

Harry took a couple of seconds, scanning the room, "You know what, you caught me, but the question is, doing what? Helping people who everyone else has either abandoned or doesn't have the means to help? Those people who took my cheap rehab, what other option did they have, stay addicted and die? Get arrested and go to jail rather than get actual treatment? Do you know how many thousands of dollars rehab costs? That's fine for celebrities, but what about most people who don't have tens of thousands of dollars lying around?"

The look on the jurors face was one of shock and intrigue, he had them captivated, hanging on his every word.

"Those guns that I shipped away, you wouldn't have been able to trace it back to the crime anyway, so isn't it better to just get them out of here? Those people who they claim I rip off, my interest rate is actually cheaper than the cheque cashing places. We actually provided financial counselling to help them get out rather than keeping them permanently indebted. I have done more to put a stop to poverty and violent crime than everyone else in this room put together. Those soldiers, the people we supposedly love and admire so much, too many of them come back with PTSD and are left to live under bridges. I got them out from under those bridges and got them to work protecting women's rights in other states."

He took one more look at Ms. James, and she looked at him with desperation, fearing the worst for him. "Let's not kid ourselves here, I'm not here because I was breaking the law, I'm here because I gave dozens of people a fighting chance in court, and gave Mr. Levine a lot more work to do – actually doing his job. That's my crime, making sure people get the trial promised to them by the constitution, all this other stuff is just a bunch of cheap excuses."

Harry then turned to Judge Reeves, "Your Honour, if I am guilty, then what does that make the cheque cashing places who take advantage of the desperate and keep them there as long as possible? What does that make the people who railroad people into prison? What does that make the people who don't help addicts but leave them to either die, or be sent to prison with violent criminals, as if one has anything to do with the other?"

Harry turned to the jury, "If you convict me, what message are you sending society? That you don't care about anyone but yourselves, that the person who risked his life multiple times to help this city should just be tossed away to serve the D. A.'s office? What if, like Walter Evans, you're the one that gets accused of a crime you didn't commit? Would he be there for you? No chance in hell. I am the person that would give you a chance in court, I am the person that this city needs, I am a lot of people's last chance."

With seemingly the entire courtroom in the palm of his hand, he finished, "Two weeks ago, Ethan Sawyer called me the devil, and maybe I am. However, when all these supposed angels abandon you, the devil's offer sounds pretty good."

He walked back to his seat next to Ms. James as the jury members looked at each other with shock, contemplating what had just been said. Without saying a word Ms. James could see them all wondering if what they just heard was the harsh truth, or the last act of a desperate and manipulative criminal.

Judge Reeves sent the jurors away to reach a verdict, Harry and Ms. James look at each other unsure if that would be enough. As the minutes went by Harry and Ms. James waited patiently in the lobby. Ms. James reached into her pocket and Harry said to her, "We're being watched, don't touch your cell phone."

Ms. James looked back at him confused, while Harry was looking at Mr. Levine from a distance on the phone.

Ms. James whispered to him, "I don't know what you're concern is but worst case scenario, I will go straight for an appeal and we can get this taken care of."

Harry said to her, "I always feared it would come to this, I tried to avoid this."

Ms. James, trying to make him feel better, said, "Don't get discouraged, we poked a lot of holes in his arguments."

The bailiff called them back to the courtroom, and as Judge Reeves sat on the bench, Mr. Levine, Ms. James and Harry all sat down at their respective tables. The jurors filed in one after another, the tension built with each passing second as they all took their seats. A middle aged juror with glasses and a moustache sat on the front seat closest to Judge Reeves.

Judge Reeves asked, "Has the jury reached their verdict?"

The closest juror stood up with a piece of paper, "We have, Your Honour. On the charge of loan sharking we find the defendant, not guilty."

There were many whispers as the judge called for silence as the lead juror, with great reluctance, declared, "On the charges of illegal gambling, prostitution, drug trafficking, illegal firearm sales, money laundering, coercion, conspiracy to commit burglary, and perjury we find the defendant guilty."

More whispers filled the courtroom, as Judge Reeves banged her gavel, demanding silence.

"Harry Goodrich, your sentencing will be determined three weeks from today and I hereby set bail at $150,000."

The dread on Harry's face was clear. Ms. James looked away from Harry to see the smirk on the face of Mr. Levine who turned on his cell phone. Suddenly seeing multiple texts and other messages, he then got a phone call and he immediately picked up as everyone was beginning to leave the courtroom. He blurted out, "What's going on?"

The voice on the other end said, "We got him he's dead, you don't have to worry about that immunity."

Mr. Levine's eyes went wide as he said, "What, are you talking about? Who's dead?"

The voice on the other end said, "Alvarez, come on you sent me an e-mail telling me we had to take him out, and the best part is you can claim you weren't involved. I'll pretend he was going to pull a gun on me and we don't have to worry anymore."

Mr. Levine yelled in the courtroom that was partially empty, "I didn't tell you to kill Alvarez, we're trying to destroy Goodrich!"

The courtroom became deadly silent, as he looked over at Harry Goodrich. "You did this, you had him killed in my office, you son of a bitch."

He furiously charged at Harry as the judge had to order the bailiff to restrain Mr. Levine.

Everyone was in a state of shock at this turn of events as Ms. James turned to him, the wheels turned in her mind realizing what Harry had just done. She whispered to him, "I thought you didn't kill, how could you do this? Maybe you are the devil."

Harry responded with a tear beginning to form in his eye, "There are no devils, there are no Gods, just people, who fight to destroy each other and try to claim places like Covenant City as their own. I tried to break the cycle, but I failed. Alvarez, Levine and I destroyed each other, now it begins all over again."

About The Author

Peter Howe was born outside of Toronto Ontario Canada in 1988.

He graduated from the University of Guelph-Humber with a Bachelor's Degree in Business Administration. While attaining his CPA Designation, he decided to branch out beyond bookkeeping and accounting to incorporate more of his interests into his life. His broad knowledge and passions contribute to his desire to write books about a variety of subjects, genres and formats.

Also by This Author

Peter Howe has other books that are currently available on Amazon and other online book sellers. These include:

The Game Changer: A Collection of Poetry (2015)

Confront the Raven (2016)

Melvoy's Railroad (2018)

More coming in the years ahead!

Made in the USA
Middletown, DE
16 April 2019